STARDUST
ACADEMY

Also by Siobhan Rowden

The Curse of the Bogle's Beard
Revenge of the Ballybogs
Wild Moose Chase

STARDUST ACADEMY

★ **SIOBHAN ROWDEN** ★

Scholastic Children's Books
An imprint of Scholastic Ltd
Euston House, 24 Eversholt Street, London, NW1 1DB, UK
Registered office: Westfield Road, Southam, Warwickshire, CV47 0RA
SCHOLASTIC and associated logos are trademarks and/or
registered trademarks of Scholastic Inc.

First published in the UK by Scholastic Ltd, 2015

Text copyright © Siobhan Rowden, 2015

The right of Siobhan Rowden to be identified as the author of this work
has been asserted by her.

ISBN 978 1407 13874 9

A CIP catalogue record for this book is available
from the British Library.

Printed by CPI Group (UK) Ltd, Croydon, CR0 4YY
Papers used by Scholastic Children's Books are made
from wood grown in sustainable forests.

1 3 5 7 9 10 8 6 4 2

This is a work of fiction. Names, characters, places, incidents and dialogues are
products of th   nce to
actual pe

For my mum,
a true "Milliken girl",
with much love.

Auditions taking place for:

STARDUST ACADEMY

The school where *"FAME means EVERYTHING!"*

Do you want to be horribly **rich?**
Do you want to be hideously **gorgeous?**
Do you want to be **loved by everybody?**
Fame will bring you all of this and more...

Here at **Stardust Academy** we will teach you how
to become famous, and lead you into the **glamorous,
glorious, glittering world of showbiz.**

All acts considered.

**Audition Date: Saturday 1st August
Time: 09:00 – 17:00
Venue: Stardust Academy Theatre**

Come and meet our celebrity founder –
all-round entertainer, living legend and national treasure

Fenella Stardust

Note: Participants must be between 11 and 12 years old. Only those with
"natural sparkle" need apply. Places are limited.

1

Happy Birthday, Me, Me, Me

Vip Locks looked at the poster that his mum was pinning to the fridge, and his heart sank.

"But I don't want to be famous," he said.

His mother swung round to face him. She was wearing one of her dresses which she'd decorated with rows of cooked sausages. Vip flinched as a frankfurter whipped past his eye.

"Don't be so ridiculous!" she snapped. "Of course you do – everyone wants to be famous! You have to live up to your name, Vip, and become a Very Important Person. Your father and I have been waiting your whole life for this audition. This is a chance for you to finally become a 'somebody'."

"But I am a 'somebody'," he murmured. "I'm *me*."

Mum shook her head, her jet-black hair falling round her shoulders in big, bouncy curls. "I mean a *real* somebody," she said. "Like me or your dad."

Vip winced as his mum carried on talking. "You're so lucky to have parents like us. I've been on the cover of all the local newspapers – everything from the *Evening Argus* to *Pig Weekly*. They're all desperate to get a photo of me in one of my celebrated sausage dresses. As for your dad – well, with a number-one hit song under his belt, everybody wants to meet Goldwin Locks. He's so excited that the auditions are coming up. Soon we can all be celebrities. The Locks dynasty! Where is he anyway? Goldwin? GOLDWIN?"

She tottered out of the large kitchen on strappy high heels. Vip sighed and sat down at the long, glass dining table. A huge TV took up the entire wall in front of him. A pop channel was pumping out loud music, and flashing images lit up the room. He wished he could turn it off but his

4

parents always left it on in case his dad's video was played. His dad had only ever had one hit record – "Happy Birthday, Me, Me, Me", a birthday song he'd written to himself. That was nearly ten years ago, but it was still sometimes played at parties and anniversaries, and very occasionally popped up on TV music channels.

Vip turned away from the television only to be faced with giant photos of his parents smiling down at him from every other wall. There was one of them opening a supermarket, cutting a red ribbon with a large pair of scissors, and another at a nightclub. His dad was playing a golden keyboard, his teeth as white as the keys. Mum was holding a tambourine, her shiny sausage dress glinting in the disco lights. There were also dozens of photos of them with famous people in the background, and a framed disc which showed how many copies of "Happy Birthday, Me, Me, Me" had been sold.

Vip put the TV on mute and breathed in the silence. He had been dreading this moment. His parents were desperate for him to go to Stardust

Academy. It was the most famously famous fame-school in the world. Every year thousands of hopeful parents and children flocked to the auditions, even though only ten places were available. Vip knew he didn't stand a chance. He couldn't sing, dance, act or anything like that, despite his parents' best efforts. But that wouldn't stop them from forcing him to take part in the audition. They were going to think of some sort of act for him to perform, and then they were going to be horribly disappointed when he failed. The idea of getting up in front of an audience made Vip feel sick. All he wanted to do was work with animals and maybe one day become a vet.

A small, squeaky meow interrupted his thoughts. "Hello, Olive," he said, as a little black cat with a beautiful shiny coat and a very long tail emerged from under the table. She rubbed against his legs before padding towards a large hamster cage in the corner of the room. "Don't wake Henry up," he whispered. "He's not ready to play yet."

Mum wobbled back through the door and

glanced at Olive. "She'll eat that hamster one of these days. You can never trust a cat."

"She won't hurt him," said Vip. "The only thing she's ever pounced on is a fairy cake. She's not like other cats. She's special."

Mum shrugged as Vip's dad came striding into the room smelling of *He-Man* aftershave. His long blonde hair was tied back in a ponytail and he was wearing an electric-blue suit. "Stardust Academy, here we come!" he boomed, slapping Vip on the back. "You're going to meet Fenella Stardust, Vip. That woman is a legend. A true celeb! She's been on the TV since we were kids."

"That's right," said Mum. "She's been around for ever, started off in a double act called Chalk and Cheese. They used to sing and dance and tell jokes."

"Then she went solo and hit the big time as Fenella Stardust," continued Dad. "What a pro! No one can wear a fur hat the way she can. This is it, Vip. This is your chance to become a star."

"Then we can have our photo taken with you!" cried Mum.

"You can do that already," said Vip.

Mum looked at him blankly. "What's the point if you're not famous?"

Vip glanced up at the wall covered in photographs. There wasn't a single picture of him. "Most parents like having photos of their children," he muttered.

"Luckily for you, we're not most parents," said Dad. "Once you've hit the big time your picture will take pride of place."

"What if I *don't* hit the big time?"

"If you get into Stardust Academy, then it's almost guaranteed."

Vip let out a long sigh and sat down on the shiny black floor. He watched as Olive attempted to wake the hamster up. She was clawing at the lock on his cage. "Would you be proud of me even if I didn't become famous?" he asked. "How would you feel if I became, say . . . a vet?"

Mum pulled a face. "Rumour has it, Fenella Stardust uses magic to make her students famous," she said, completely ignoring Vip's question.

Vip had seen Fenella Stardust on TV a few times,

and the only magical thing about her was that her forehead remained mysteriously immobile despite what the rest of her face was doing.

"We're going to need a bit of magic to get this one through the auditions," said Dad, looking down at Vip. "What's he going to do? It's in two weeks' time, and he can't *do* anything."

"Mr Clarke says I'm good at maths," said Vip. "I got an A in algebra and—"

"What good will maths do you?" sniffed Mum. "Although there is that TV programme where the presenter has to add and subtract and ... weird things like that. What's it called again?"

"*Count-up*," said Dad. "But he couldn't even do that. Look how skinny he is. He doesn't stand out at all – no stage presence. I don't know why you won't let us dye your hair blonde, Vip. Brown is so boring, and it does nothing to help your ... disorder."

Vip shook his head and looked at Olive. She had managed to unlock the cage and was now prodding the sleepy hamster with her nose. "I don't think being shy is a disorder," he said. "Mr Clarke says as I get older, I'll find it easier to talk to people. He says as long as I work hard and I'm kind and considerate, that's all that really matters."

"Oh, Mr Clarke says this and Mr Clarke says that," grumbled Mum. "Whoever heard of anyone becoming famous because they were kind?"

"There was the Good Samaritan," said Dad, thoughtfully, ". . . and Mother Theresa of course, but I'm not sure Vip would make a very good nun. We need to think."

They all watched as the hamster ran out of the cage and Olive dashed in, shutting the door with her paw. Vip picked the hamster up and tickled his tummy. "Hello, Henry," he whispered. "I know *you* will still love me even if I don't become famous, but what about them?"

Dad sat down beside Vip and put his arm around his shoulders. "I know I'm a hard act to follow, son," he said. "Talent like mine is rare. But look at your mother. She changed her name from plain old Sally to Salami, and managed to get into the newspapers just by wearing sausage dresses. And boy, does she sizzle!"

Mum giggled and did a little twirl. "I could make Vip a small sausage suit," she said. "He could be known as 'Chipolata Boy' and—"

She stopped mid-sentence and pointed up at the huge television, gasping loudly. "It's on! It's on, Goldwin! Your song's on TV!"

Dad jumped to his feet and lunged towards the remote control. "Who muted the telly?" he roared, desperately tapping all the buttons.

Suddenly the sound of Dad's deep voice blared from the eight speakers dotted around the room.

> *Every year I'm looking better,*
> *Fighting fit, a real go-getter,*
> *Muscles, charm and looks collide,*
> *Gorgeousness personified.*
>
> *Happy Birthday, Me, Me, Me,*
> *I have a special chemistry,*
> *It's hard to be beyond compare,*
> *A face like mine is oh so rare.*

11

So every year I celebrate,
That happy mid-November date,
The world got me – you lucky lot,
Handsome, smart and smokin' hot!

Happy Birthday, Me, Me, Me,
I'm so awesome, as you see,
I have no blackheads, spots or pimples,
Just great hair, white teeth and dimples.

Vip watched as his parents danced round the kitchen, singing along to the repeating chorus. Dad released his ponytail and whooshed his hair over one shoulder, flashing a brilliant smile as he belted out the last line. At the end of the song they struck a familiar pose – one that Vip had seen in hundreds of photos. Dad with his legs apart and hands on his hips, with Mum draped over his left shoulder, one knee held high, pouting at an imaginary audience.

"And the crowd goes wild!" bellowed Dad.

Vip looked around the room. Henry the hamster had disappeared into his top pocket, trembling fearfully, and Olive had covered her ears with her paws. Vip fished out the shaking hamster and tried to open his cage, as his parents relaxed their pose with lots of high fiving and cheers.

"That's how you do it, son," said Dad, a bead of perspiration running down his smooth forehead. "Watch and learn, watch and learn. . ."

Vip nodded distractedly and continued trying to open the hamster cage. "I've got a problem," he said.

Mum immediately flopped down beside him and gave his hand a squeeze. "We know, darling. But you won't always be a nobody."

"That is not the problem!" he spluttered. "I can't get the cage open. Olive has locked herself in."

They all knelt down and peered into the cage. Olive was squashed in a corner purring happily.

"There used to be a small key," he continued. "But I lost it ages ago, so I never lock the door properly any more. But Olive has somehow managed to lock it with her claw. How am I going to get her out?"

Suddenly, Olive reached out a long, elegant paw

13

and began to fiddle with the lock. Seconds later the door swung open and she strolled out of the cage and back under the table. Mum and Dad watched open-mouthed.

"Am I seeing things, or did that cat just pick a lock?" asked Dad.

"She's a genius," gasped Mum.

Vip nodded. "I told you she was special."

"Wait!" cried Dad. "This is it! This is what we've been looking for. Vip can perform with Olive. We've just found ourselves an act – The Amazing Cat Burglars!"

2

Fenella Stardust

Two weeks later. . .

Vip stood at the front of a long queue, looking through a set of golden gates. A large, sparkling sign sat proudly on top:

Stardust Academy

On the other side of the gates was a sweeping drive which wound its way up a steep hill to a giant star-shaped building. Two of the star's points were rooted firmly on the ground, two stretched out east and west and a fifth pointed towards the sky to form an enormous pentagram. It was made of glass, which flashed in the morning sun. When he first saw the academy Vip thought it looked like a real star that had fallen to earth and landed on top of the hill. But twelve hours later, his initial amazement had turned to boredom. Mum and Dad had insisted that they leave the night before and camp in front of the gates so that they would be first in line for the auditions. Their two-man tent, which all three of them had to sleep in, was now packed away, and Vip was dressed in a skintight black catsuit with a fluffy tail, an eye mask and a pair of pointy ears. Mum had painted his nose black and given him some whiskers. A small child walked past and pointed at him.

"Look, Mummy! A ballet-dancing Batman!"

Vip felt his face burn and was suddenly grateful for his mask. He tried to hide behind his dad. "Can I at least put my coat on till we get in?" he asked.

"No. You need to get into character," said Dad.

"And you look sooooo cute," added Mum, tickling him behind one of his furry ears.

Vip shook her off and glanced anxiously around him. "I'm eleven years old – I don't want to look cute," he complained. "This is the worst day of my whole life! And Olive isn't happy either."

He looked down at the wicker cat carrier. It was secured with black tape. They had tried to lock the door but she kept getting out. A plaintive *meow* escaped from inside. Vip bent down and poked a piece of cheese through a gap before turning back to his parents. "Please don't make me audition. I look ridiculous and everyone is staring."

"I think you'll find they're staring at me," said Dad, stepping out of the queue and waving at the long line of children and parents waiting for the auditions to start. "Hi, guys! Goldwin Locks here!"

There was a moment of silence as everyone stared at him. Dad pulled the collar up on his cropped leather jacket and looked over the top of his sunglasses. "Happy Birthday, Me, Me, Me?" he prompted.

17

Suddenly, everybody erupted in whoops of excitement.

"Look!" shouted the ecstatic crowd. "Look who it is!" They all began to surge forward.

"Yes, it's me!" boomed Dad. He stood with his arms out in welcome, and was just about to release his ponytail when he realized that the people were running past him and pressing themselves against the huge golden gates.

"It's her! It's Fenella Stardust!" shouted another child's mum, pushing Dad out of the way. "She's coming down the drive. Fenella, Fenella! We love you, Fenella!"

Vip found himself squeezed against the gates next to his mum. "They're squashing my sausages," she gasped.

He managed to turn his head and look between the golden railings. A long, white limousine was driving down the hill, and Fenella Stardust was rising out of the sunroof. She was wearing one of her trademark fur hats even though it was a warm summer's day. Her dazzling white suit glittered in the sunshine, and as she got closer, Vip saw that it was encrusted with thousands of tiny crystals. She held her hands up in the air and smiled broadly, revealing teeth so white that several people had to put their sunglasses on. Even Vip had to admit she was an impressive sight.

"Fenella! Fenella! Fenella!" chanted the crowd.

Dad came elbowing his way through them, pouting indignantly. "Out of the way, you rabble. We were here first."

"Goldwin," cried Mum. "Look at her – isn't she wonderful? Her teeth are even whiter than yours."

Dad stared at Fenella Stardust. "Fake gnashers, pumped-up lips and a forehead as solid as concrete," he said. "There's no denying it – that woman has style! She must be at least sixty, but looks half that."

The limousine approached the gates and came to a stop. Fenella Stardust was still smiling broadly. Everything about her seemed to glitter – her suit, her teeth, even her tanned skin. Vip noticed a diamond-encrusted star dangling from her neck. "Welcome!

Welcome! Welcome to Stardust Academy!" she shouted.

The crowd went wild. Fenella Stardust nodded appreciatively and briefly closed her eyes as if she were absorbing the applause.

"Who wants to be famous?" she bellowed.

"We do!" screamed the crowd.

"What does fame mean?"

"EVERYTHING!" they cheered.

"That's right, and I'm ready to see YOU sparkle!"

She pointed a long, manicured finger at the crowd. Vip felt sure she was pointing directly at him, and instinctively shrank back.

"In just one moment, your gateway to fame will open," said Fenella Stardust, nodding towards the golden gates, "and I'd like you to dance, prance or simply strut your stuff up the hill to Stardust Academy. I'm looking forward to meeting all you boys and girls, and mums, dads and guardians inside the theatre."

To Vip's relief the limo began to turn. A small man with floppy black hair, dressed in black ballet tights and a dinner jacket, jumped out before the car headed back up the hill. Fenella Stardust gave a final wave and disappeared back inside, the top of her white fur hat still poking out of the sunroof. The man produced a megaphone as the golden gates swung open.

"Hello, darlings!" he shouted, flicking his hair out of his eye. "I am Mr Poser-Prince, the dance master here at Stardust Academy and the man in charge of the auditions. Yes, yes, I am. Please come through the gates in an orderly line and follow me up the hill to the academy. As the brilliant and utterly gorgeous Fenella Stardust has mentioned, you may dance your way up. Ballroom, Latin, tap, ballet, hip hop and morris are all encouraged. If however, you are unable to do any of these, then I want to see those jazz hands. Remember – I may be watching you!"

Slowly, the long queue of people began to surge through the gates towards Mr Poser-Prince. Vip looked around in surprise as children and parents began pirouetting and cha-cha-cha-ing up the hill.

He watched in alarm as Dad began clicking his fingers and swinging his head in time to his steps as he followed Mr Poser-Prince. Mum was right behind him shimmying her sausages. "Come on, Vip," she cried. "Keep up. We don't want to lose our place in the line."

Vip scuttled behind them, terrified that people were watching. But everyone seemed more concerned with their own steps. A girl behind him was waltzing along, continuously counting to three. Her father kept accidently hitting Vip's tail with his wiggling jazz hands. Mr Poser-Prince was skipping along at the front like the Pied Piper.

"Fabulous!" he cried through the megaphone. "Fab-u-lous! But be careful, darlings. Everyone must stay on the path. Anyone caught stepping on the grass or jumping the queue will not be auditioned. Ms Stardust is very particular about good manners."

Vip shuffled along behind his parents, staring at the ground. As they got closer to the academy, he realized that the enormous star was actually just a facade. Attached to the back of the glass pentagram

22

stood a rather boring brick building. Mr Poser-Prince led them under the two pointed legs of the star to a set of double doors which opened up into the school behind.

"OK, darlings" he bellowed. "We are now about to enter the academy. I ask that each and every one of you observe and respect our basic school rules. No running in the corridors, although shimmying, flouncing and moonwalking are all acceptable. No drinks other than bottled spring water from the Swiss Alps, no food other than faddy diets, no dirty fingernails and absolutely no greasy hair. Fenella Stardust is meticulous when it comes to personal hygiene and cleanliness."

Vip looked down at his hands. His fingernails were quite grubby and he knew that underneath Olive's beautiful sleek, black coat, she suffered from a bit of catty-dandruff. There was no way they would get through. Part of him was relieved, though he'd still have his parents' disappointment to put up with.

They followed Mr Poser-Prince through the

doors into a long, bright corridor. It was lined with huge photographs of smiling people. Vip recognized some of them from the glossy magazines his mum loved reading. She was getting very excited.

"These are all celebrities who have graduated from Stardust Academy," she gasped. "There's that opera singer from the telly. Not my cup of tea, but at least she's famous. Ooh, look! There's Chardonnay Frontage! She's famous for ... erm ... well, being famous, I think. She's in all the magazines, anyway. And there's Steven Stolid. He was on that reality show where everyone had to suck their own toes for fourteen days. He was brilliant! Vip, you could be just like him!"

Vip stared straight ahead and kept on walking. His stomach was churning madly. The auditions were very close now and he was going to have to get up on a stage and perform. He could hear his dad trying to get Mr Poser-Prince's attention.

"Goldwin Locks, here, Mr Poser-Prince," he said, quickening his pace to catch him up. "You might remember me from 'Happy Birthday, Me, M—'"

"Fabulous, darling," said Mr Poser-Prince. "But I'm afraid there's no time for chit-chat."

They finally came to a set of heavy velvet curtains. Mr Poser-Prince pulled a thick purple cord and the curtains slid back to reveal a large auditorium. Tiers of seating led down to an enormous stage. Mr Poser-Prince handed Vip a number to pin on his catsuit. "You are number one," he said, picking up a clipboard. "Name, please?"

Vip opened his mouth to speak but nothing came out. His throat was dry and he was afraid he might be sick on Mr Poser-Prince's ballet pumps. He backed off and tried to hide behind his mum.

"What's wrong?" asked Mr Poser-Prince.

"He's a bit shy," Mum replied.

Mr Poser-Prince drew in a sharp breath of air and took a step back as though Vip had measles.

"I'm afraid we don't do *shy* here!"

"He's not shy," cried Dad, thrusting Vip in front of him. "What my wife means is that he's . . . *shi-ny*."

Mr Poser-Prince looked doubtful. "Shiny?" he repeated.

"Like a star," said Dad. "His name is Vip, V-I-P, because that is what he's going to be – a Very Important Person just like his dad. Did I mention I'm Goldwin Locks? 'Happy Birth—'"

"Yes, several times, darling," said Mr Poser-Prince, scribbling on his clipboard. "OK, take a seat. Next!"

Mum pulled Vip down an aisle towards the stage. Dad followed grumbling quietly. "That man doesn't know his celebs from his slobs," he muttered.

Vip closed his eyes and allowed himself to be dragged to the front row of the stalls. He could hear the seats around him being taken. "Do we have to perform in front of everyone? I thought it would just be the judges."

"No, the whole theatre will be full," said Mum. "Isn't that exciting?"

Vip shuddered and tried to forget about where he was. He imagined that he was in his room at home, playing with the hamster. "I am not here, and this is not happening," he whispered.

"Look at him, Sal," said Dad. "He's visualizing

26

his performance. Mentally, he is up on that stage already. Well done, son."

Slowly the auditorium filled up and became very noisy. There were singers practising their scales, kids in sparkling leotards walking past on their hands, and various hoots and blasts coming from all sorts of instruments. Vip was nudged forward as someone sat down in the seats behind them.

"Goldwin Locks?" asked a voice.

Dad's eyes lit up. "A fan!" he said.

They all turned round to face a smart lady in a trouser suit sitting down next to a girl of about the same age as Vip. Dad's face fell. It was their neighbour. "Oh, it's only you, Mrs Milliken. What are you doing here?"

"Same as you, of course," said the lady. "You didn't think I would miss out on a chance like this with my Melody, did you? There's no doubt she'll win a place. We Milliken girls can do anything, you know."

The girl looked at Vip and rolled her enormous green eyes. Her long red hair was topped with a stripy bobble hat and she was clutching a violin. "Hi, Vip."

Vip stared back at Melody Milliken. They lived on the same road, and even though he wanted to, he could never quite manage to say hello. This was his chance but he was dressed like a ballet-dancing Batman. *Say something*, he thought. *Anything*.

"I'm a cat," he blurted.

Melody nodded slowly. "That's nice."

"Oh, look at his whiskers, Melody," said Mrs Milliken. "Doesn't he look … sweet? I suppose you're going to do some sort of novelty act? Of course, my Melody will be performing a little something from Vivaldi's *Four Seasons*. She's been practising hard and I'm happy to say that we are now note-perfect."

Melody glanced up at Vip and gave a tiny shake of her head. He couldn't help smiling.

"It hasn't been easy, though," continued Mrs Milliken. "There have been a few arguments. I only ask that she practises for four hours before school and five hours after. How else is she going to be a world-famous musician?"

"I could give her a few tips," said Dad.

Mrs Milliken peered at him over the top of her glasses. "Hmm ... have you opened any more supermarkets recently, Mr Locks?"

"I've got a few gigs lined up," he answered. "Sal and I are hosting the 'sing-along-to-an-annoying-old-song night' at the village hall next Wednesday. And I'm writing my autobiography, *But Enough About You – Let's Talk About Me.*"

"How interesting."

"Yes, I am, and I want to share that with the world. It's just not fair keeping me to myself, so—"

"Another unusual dress, Mrs Locks," continued Mrs Milliken, completely ignoring Dad. "One of your own creations, I take it?"

"No," said Mum, jumping from her chair and twirling round. "It's a designer dress – a McCartney."

"Ooh, Stella?"

"No – Linda. These are veggie sausages."

They stopped talking as a ripple of applause trickled through the crowd. Vip looked up to see

Mr Poser-Prince climbing the steps on to the stage and switching on a microphone.

"May I have your attention please," he said. "The auditions are now ready to commence in numerical order. Please listen out for your personal number and make your way on to the stage. But first of all, please put your hands together for the most fabulous woman in showbiz. The one and only, MS FENELLA STARDUST!"

A giant screen at the back of the stage lit up to the sound of loud dramatic music. Hundreds of different coloured lights zoomed back and forth, almost hypnotizing the audience before eventually settling into large flashing letters:

FENELLASTARDUSTFENELLASTARDUST

She came sweeping on to the stage, a huge smile plastered across her heavily made-up face. She was now dressed in a sparkling red dress with giant shoulder pads and a matching cape. Her white fur hat had been replaced with a black one. She held her hands up to her ears for the crowd to cheer louder, then covered them in fake surprise when they did. Her enormous white teeth flashed under the spotlights which gleamed down from above. She took off her hat, revealing a short crop of spiky black hair, and waved it at the audience before replacing it and grabbing the microphone.

"What does fame mean?" she shouted.

"EVERYTHING!" returned the ecstatic audience.

"You'd better believe it! And today some of YOU will be picked to experience the glory! Ten talented children selected from these auditions will win a place at Stardust Academy starting this September."

The sound in the auditorium was deafening. Vip covered his ears and closed his eyes as Fenella Stardust made her way over to a large desk surrounded by light bulbs. It took up one side of the whole stage.

"Helping me today on the judging panel will be some of the finest teaching staff in the world – my heads of department. Starting with Mr Quentin Poser-Prince, Head of Dance!"

Everyone applauded as he took a seat next to Fenella Stardust.

"Also, Miss Ivana Maykova, Head of Image!"

A tall, glamorous lady with long blonde hair and enormous red lips sat on her other side.

"Head of Music – Mr Ludwig Van Driver!"

A portly old man waved to everyone before sitting down.

"And finally," shouted Fenella Stardust, "give it up for Mr Mason Robust, Head of PE, Health and Fitness!"

The clapping continued as a huge triangle of a man sat on the final chair behind the desk. "So, without further ado, let the auditions begin!"

The crowd roared as Mr Poser-Prince checked his clipboard.

"Will number one please take to the stage?" he shouted above the noise. "Vip Locks."

The applause washed over Vip like a cold shower. He was finding it hard to breathe and the palms of his hands were soaking wet. He looked around frantically but there was nowhere to hide.

3

The Audition

"Vip, it's you!" shouted Dad. "Get up there. It's time to make us proud. Why do you think we named you Vip?"

"Because I'm a very important person ... to you?" he asked, hopefully.

Dad looked confused. "You're not famous yet, son."

Vip closed his eyes and swallowed deeply. "I c-can't. I'm going to be sick. P-please don't make me."

"Nerves are a good thing," said Mum, hauling him out of his seat and thrusting the cat basket at him. "I'll help you with the props."

She grabbed a large box made from clear plastic with a red padlock dangling from a catch on one side, and dragged him up the steps on to the stage.

"Hurry up, please," barked Mr Poser-Prince. "We have lots of people to get through."

Vip clutched the cat basket close to him and stared down at his feet. He couldn't bring himself to look out at the packed auditorium.

"Open it," said Mum.

He peeled off the black tape around the basket with trembling fingers. Olive sauntered out of the small door, her gleaming fur shining like a black pearl. Vip thought he heard Fenella Stardust give a little gasp. Olive glanced contemptuously at the judges and then at the audience in front of her.

"D-don't be s-scared, Olive," Vip stuttered, picking her up.

"She's not the one who's wobbling like a jelly," whispered Mum, handing him the clear box. "Now, pull yourself together and start singing!"

Olive climbed up on to Vip's shoulder as he

placed the clear box on the desk in front of the judges. Fenella Stardust smiled encouragingly.

"We haven't got all day, darling," said Mr Poser-Prince. "Will you please begin your act?"

Vip faced the audience and opened his mouth to sing the song that his dad had written for him. His fluffy tail was quivering violently and the faces in front of him began to sway and merge together. He stared at the crowd, his mind completely blank.

"We are the cat burglars..." prompted Mum from the side of the stage.

"W-we are the cat b-burglars," croaked Vip, "we are on a mission. We are the cat burglars, with our night vision ... erm ... we ... um..."

"Sing it, don't say it," said Mum.

"S-sing it, don't say it," repeated Vip.

"No!" cried Mum.

There were a few sniggers from the audience. Vip could just make out his dad's blonde head shaking in disbelief. "Forget the song," he hissed. "Go straight to the main act."

A wave of nausea swept through Vip's body, and

his stomach gurgled loudly. He turned to the panel. "H-has anyone got anything valuable they would like to keep safe from the cat burglars?" he asked in a small voice.

"We can't hear him!" shouted someone in the crowd.

Dad stood up and turned around to face them. "Listen more carefully!" he yelled.

Fenella Stardust smiled at Vip and handed him her own diamond-encrusted watch. There was a collective gasp. Vip could see his mum bouncing up and down in excitement, her sausages flying everywhere. He took the watch and placed it inside the plastic box. He then closed the padlock with a small key and glanced back at Mum.

"Go on – say it," she urged.

"W-would you like to try and open the box?" he asked.

Fenella Stardust fiddled with the lock. "It looks secure to me," she said. "Would you agree, Miss Maykova?"

The glamorous teacher beside her pulled the

door and then nodded in agreement. Vip took Olive from his shoulder and placed her on the desk. He had forgotten what he was supposed to say again and he was very aware of the rumbles coming from his stomach.

"But nothing is safe. . ." whispered Mum.

"B-but nothing is safe . . . from the cat burglars," he mumbled.

Olive approached the box, stretched out her paw and began fiddling with the lock. Fenella Stardust watched her closely. Vip couldn't help noticing that Olive looked just like Fenella Stardust's hat. A minute later the door of the box swung open and Olive grabbed the watch in her mouth and delivered it to Vip. The judges' eyes widened and the audience began clapping. Fenella Stardust got to her feet and joined in with the applause as Vip handed her back her watch. It was all over, but the relief flooding through him only made his stomach feel worse.

"Well done!" cried Fenella Stardust. "That cat is unique – such confidence, such grace, such intelligence, such ... a beautiful coat. Cats are usually very hard to train, but this one is jam-packed with natural talent. What's it called?"

"O-Olive," he managed.

"Olive," she repeated, staring intently at the cat. "Olive ... hmm ... has anyone else got a question?"

Vip felt his stomach spasm, and leant against the judges' desk.

"Velcome, young man," said Miss Maykova in a thick accent. "Your cat is obviously a natural performer, but vot about you? How much do *you* vont to become famous? Vot does being here today mean to you?"

Vip looked her straight in the eye and then vomited in her lap.

4

The Winners

The next few minutes were a blur. Vip vaguely remembered Miss Maykova running off the stage screaming. This terrified Olive who leapt on top of Mr Ludwig Van Driver and scratched his nose. She then ran up the stage curtains and refused to come down. Luckily there was an acrobatic team in the audience who formed a giant pyramid and eventually brought her back down safely. This had meant a delay for everyone else, and despite Dad offering to sing to them while they waited, nobody was very happy with Vip. He sat in a cubicle in the boys' toilets with his head in his hands. The experience had been even more terrible than he could have ever imagined. He looked up at the sound of a small knock on the outside door.

"Vip?" called a voice.

He froze. It was Melody Milliken. "I know you're in there," she said. "I just want you to know that I get really nervous too. . ."

There was an awkward silence. He wanted to say something but couldn't.

"Anyway," she said, eventually. "I liked your act. . ."

Just say, thank you, he thought.

"It's my turn to audition now . . . I have to go. My mum will be going crazy . . . bye."

Vip listened to the sound of her fading footsteps. "Bye, Melody," he whispered.

Why couldn't he just talk to her? She was going to think that he was really rude. He had to get back into the auditorium and watch her perform, even if it meant facing all those people again. He left the toilets and stood beside the velvet curtains that opened up into the theatre. Slowly he walked down the side aisle towards his seat at the front. He was sure that everyone would be pointing at him, but actually they were all either chatting to each other or watching the act performing on stage. It was a pair of very small ballroom dancers. The girl wore a huge pink dress and the boy was in a matching skintight sequinned shirt and flared trousers. For a moment, Vip didn't feel quite so bad about his catsuit. His mum grabbed his arm as he sat down beside her.

"There you are, Vip. We've been worried about you," she said. "Are you feeling a bit better? Listen, we're still in with a chance. Miss Maykova has changed her outfit and is back on the panel. Apparently she has ten different outfits for today anyway. No harm done. Dad offered to give her a signed copy of 'Happy Birthday, Me, Me, Me', and I said that if there were any stains on her clothes, I could sew on some sausages to hide them. She declined both offers and said it was perfectly all right. I said you had food poisoning."

"Is Olive OK?" he asked. "And where's Dad?"

"Olive's fast asleep in her basket and Dad is signing some autographs."

Vip turned round to see his dad crouching in the aisle talking to an old lady with a walking stick and a hearing aid who was there with her grandson. "But, I don't want to buy any ice cream," she was saying.

"I'm not selling anything," said Dad in a loud voice. "I'm trying to give you my autograph."

"No, I'm not having a laugh," she sighed. "But I'll buy two tubs of vanilla if you leave me alone."

Vip cringed. Why was his dad so desperate to be loved by everyone – anyone? He sighed and turned back to look at Fenella Stardust who was watching the tiny ballroom dancers. Her orange skin was scraped back across her face, pulling the ends of her mouth into a large set smile.

"Doesn't that little boy look fabulous?" said Mum, pointing up at the stage. "A sparkly outfit like that would be great for your school discos. It would help with your confidence – make you stand out."

"It would make me stand out, all right," whispered Vip.

The small girl did a final twirl and curtseyed to the audience as the boy gave a curt bow. The judges made some notes, and there was a smattering of applause. The more acts there were, the less attentive everyone was. *If only I hadn't gone first,* he thought.

"Ooh!" cried Mum. "Here comes Melody."

Vip watched Melody walking up the steps. Mrs Milliken was right behind her, holding her hands up for silence. "Could everyone please be quiet!" she shouted. "I will not have any distractions during my daughter's performance. I don't want Ms Stardust to miss a thing."

She smiled over at the judges. Fenella Stardust had her fixed smile at the ready. The other teachers just stared back at her.

"You at the back – stop talking," Mrs Milliken continued. "Yes, you in the hippo costume ... oh, it's not a costume. Well, pay attention anyway."

A hush descended in the theatre. Dad came

43

creeping back to his chair as Melody held her violin up to her chin. Vip could see her hands trembling as she placed them on the strings. He crossed his fingers and toes, willing her to do well.

As the first notes drifted across the stage, Vip realized that Mrs Milliken didn't need to get everyone's attention beforehand. The music was beautiful, and every eye and ear in the house was focused on Melody. Vip could see that her initial nervousness evaporated with every note. She dipped and swayed as if she were part of the music. Vip was mesmerized. He had never heard anything like this before. This was real talent. Eventually, Melody finished the piece to a standing ovation. She gave a small bow before running down the stage steps to her seat. Vip turned to face her, his shyness forgotten.

"That was brilliant!" he cried. "You actually should be famous. Then everybody could hear you play."

He stopped suddenly and felt the colour seep into his cheeks. But Melody smiled back. They both looked up at the stage where Mrs Milliken was bowing and waving as if she had just performed.

"Thank you, thank you," she called. "I have been working very hard to achieve this."

Vip glanced back at Melody. "I did a bit of work too," she whispered.

Eventually, Mr Poser-Prince managed to remove Mrs Milliken from the stage, and a yodelling boy began to perform.

For the rest of the day Vip had to sit through many acts including bouncing belly-dancers, synchronized goldfish, girl bands, boy bands and an old-man band called No Direction who had come to the wrong audition.

After six long hours, Fenella Stardust, who had been having regular make-up and hair breaks, came to the front of the stage holding a glittering clipboard. Everyone was fed up with applauding by now but she still got a loud cheer.

"Thank you all," she said. "This has been a truly inspirational day. But now it is time to announce the ten lucky winners who will gain a place at Stardust Academy."

The audience held their breath. It was so quiet you could hear a sequin drop.

"In no particular order," she continued, "Melody Milliken – musician."

Mrs Milliken let out a loud squawk, making Vip jump. He looked round to see Melody being crushed by her mother, her stripy bobble hat poking up from a tangle of arms. Vip glanced over at his own parents. They were sitting on the edge of their seats, willing his name to be read out.

"Dwayne Pipes – opera singer," continued Fenella Stardust. "Gunter Gruber – yodeller, Pineapple Bunting – ballet dancer, Howl Lafter – comedian, Merlin McGandalf – magician, Cherry Dropp – all-round entertainer, Ben Dee – acrobat and Perry Winkle – ventriloquist."

There were loud shouts of joy from various places around the auditorium. Everyone else applauded politely. Vip breathed a sigh of relief, then looked nervously over at his parents. Dad was on his feet glaring accusingly at the judges.

"Hold on," he shouted. "That's only nine places."

"Ah," said Fenella Stardust. "There is a slight complication with the final place. We would like to offer it to an animal rather than a person. The last place goes to Olive the cat . . . but *not* her handler."

Mum and Dad looked at each other in confusion. Vip's hands and feet went numb as Mr Poser-Prince took over the microphone.

"Could everybody else please exit the auditorium?" he said.

Vip clutched Olive close and watched as the theatre slowly emptied. The small ballroom dancer in the large pink dress was dragged out of the exit screaming and kicking. "But I want to be famous!" she screeched.

Mr Poser-Prince looked down at her from the stage. "Then you must practise those heel turns, darling," he said. "Now, could all the successful candidates please come forward? Ms Stardust needs to talk to you before we can proceed any further."

Nine very excited children stepped up on to the stage, closely followed by their even more excited parents.

"You are all very talented performers," said Fenella Stardust, smiling round at the children, "with lots of natural sparkle. But before any contracts are signed, I would like to make it extremely clear that every one of our pupils must shine like stars. Cleanliness is of the utmost importance here at Stardust Academy. We do not tolerate dirt of any kind. No dust, rust, muck, yuck, soil, oil, gunk, junk, mud, crud or belly-button fluff is allowed. A high level of personal hygiene is required before entry. However, the school does supply nail-dazzlers, hair-vacuumers, nose-shiners and teeth-whiteners."

Everybody nodded enthusiastically.

"Mr Poser-Prince," she continued, "can I ask you to check the new students' hands and fingernails while I personally check their hair? I will then talk to our feline friends down here." She pointed at Vip and Olive.

Vip watched as Fenella Stardust peered closely at

all the children's scalps before nodding in approval and making her way towards them. Olive climbed up on to Vip's shoulder and hissed. Dad stepped forward and offered his hand.

"I'm Goldwin Locks," he said. "It's a pleasure to meet you, Ms Stardust. This is my wife, Salami. We're big fans. I'm in the business myself – writer/singer/producer of 'Happy Birthday, Me, Me, Me'."

Fenella Stardust was staring at Olive, but turned her attention to Dad. "I know that song," she smiled. "We are fellow performers."

Dad's face glowed. "Yes we are! My song was number one for three weeks, and I also—"

"I want your cat," interrupted Fenella Stardust. Her gaze had returned to Olive.

Vip backed away. He didn't like the way Fenella Stardust was looking at her.

"Well, she's my son's cat actually," said Mum. "We would be delighted to have a celebrity pet, but..."

She trailed off as Fenella Stardust reached for Olive. She grabbed her and held her high in the air, looking intensely at her glossy fur. "What a coat," she murmured. "And look at that tail. I've never seen one quite as long or thick."

Vip's eyes flicked from Olive to Fenella Stardust's hat. "She has dandruff," he stated, trying to snatch her back.

"I can see she has ... dandruff," said Fenella Stardust, lifting her out of his reach. "But that can be remedied. I simply have to have her. If it's about money ... ?"

"I wouldn't sell her for all the money in the world," spluttered Vip. "She doesn't like strangers. She needs me!"

As if she was listening to every word he said, Olive suddenly lashed out at Fenella Stardust's cheek, her sharp claws extended. The woman screamed as Olive jumped out of her arms and back into Vip's.

"My face!" she screeched. "She's scratched my multi-million-pound face!"

As everyone surrounded the wailing Fenella Stardust, Vip put Olive back into her carrier and ran for the door. But a huge man stepped in their way.

Vip looked up at the square jaw of Mr Robust, Head of Health and Fitness. "Not so fast," the teacher boomed.

He marched them back to where Fenella Stardust stood. Mum was studying her wound. "It's just a graze," she said. "Nothing to worry about."

Fenella Stardust glared at Vip as they came forward, and then bared her large teeth to form the biggest, falsest smile Vip had ever seen.

"It's not a problem at all," she crooned, "I think we're all overreacting. If my face is fine then I am fine. Forgive me for being so … enthusiastic, but when I saw Olive I couldn't believe my eyes. She has so much … potential. So if she will only perform with the boy then I am happy to offer you *both* a place."

Vip felt his insides turn to ice. But there was nothing he could do but watch his parents jump up and down and scream with delight.

5

The Welcome Dinner Gala

It was a cool September evening. August had flown by, and despite pleading with his parents, Vip was once again standing outside Stardust Academy. The large pentagram was lit up, sending shafts of starlight into the air. Vip looked up and shivered. He was wearing a gold blazer, silver trousers and a white shirt. His pink tie was embroidered with the initials SA in sparkling sequins. The Stardust Academy school uniform had cost his mum and dad a small fortune but they were happy to pay it. They were standing either side of him. Vip could almost feel their elation. Dad had tonged his hair into loose curls and Mum's sausages were from the supermarket's finest range. Olive was lying across Vip's shoulders, fast asleep. They were surrounded by the other winning children and their families. Everyone was babbling excitedly. Melody and her mother were there, along with two other boys who Vip remembered from the auditions. One was a very short opera singer, Dwayne Pipes. His neat black hair was parted at the side and greased back. His father looked exactly the same but had a trimmed moustache. Vip could hear Dwayne singing to himself.

"I can't wait, I'm so excited,
Can't believe I've been invited,
Gosh, I hope that I don't spoil it,
Dad, I really need the toilet."

The other boy was Merlin McGandalf, a magician. He was nervously twiddling a short stick between his fingers. Green sparks flew out of both ends with every turn. Vip was sure that he could see the beginnings of a wispy white beard on the boy's chin. One girl was cartwheeling round and round the group. She stopped right in front of Vip. "Hi, I'm Cherry Dropp," she squealed. "This is going to be the most fabulistic, marvelistic, fantastistic experience EVER!"

Vip took a step back as she whirled off again. She nearly rolled into Mr Poser-Prince who was now standing in front of the doors. He was bathed in a shaft of white light coming from the pentagram above. Vip half expected him to be "beamed up" at any moment.

Mr Poser-Prince pulled a pocket watch out of the breast pocket of his dinner jacket and frowned. "It's five minutes past eight," he huffed, flicking his hair violently. "We're still waiting for one more student. He's late . . . ah, at last."

He pointed down the hill. Vip turned to see a boy with a cloud of dark, frizzy hair and thick-rimmed glasses racing towards them. He appeared to be wearing a surgical mask that covered his mouth, and was holding a wooden puppet which was a miniature version of himself. He was accompanied by a woman who Vip guessed was his mother.

"Perry Winkle!" shouted Mr Poser-Prince. "Late on your first day! This is extremely un-fab-u-lous!"

"We are so sorry," puffed his mother as they joined the group. "I couldn't find Perry's moon cream."

She squeezed a pea-sized lump of cream out of a tube and began vigorously rubbing it on her son's nose. "Moon cream – factor twenty-five," she said. "Perry's skin is extremely sensitive to moonlight, torchlight, starlight and candlelight. I just hope he remembers to do it himself when I'm not here."

Vip could see that behind his surgical mask, Perry's dark skin had turned a russet red.

"And he must keep his mask on," his mother continued, "in case he has a nasty reaction to any airborne dust, floating mites or wafting wheat particles."

She smelled the air and looked nervously around as if they were just about to be attacked by a wafting wheat particle. Mr Poser-Prince pursed his thin lips and cleared his throat.

"Well, now we are all here, I would like to

welcome you to your first term at Stardust Academy."

The small group erupted in cries of joy and delight. Cherry Dropp was screaming so loudly she almost fainted, and had to blow into a paper bag to calm herself down.

"We always start our new school year with a welcome dinner gala for our students and their families," continued Mr Poser-Prince. "The magnificent and totally wonderful Fenella Stardust is waiting for us with the rest of the school in our in-house restaurant – The Holly. Please step inside and leave your bags here in reception. They will be taken to your dormitories which we will show you after dinner."

Vip could hear his mum squeaking in excitement as they followed Mr Poser-Prince into the school and down a maze of corridors to a large canopied door with two potted holly bushes either side. The green canopy had The Holly emblazoned in red letters over the top. An ancient doorman dressed in a long dark coat with brass buttons lifted his smart cap in the air as they approached. "Good evening, Mr Poser-Prince," he croaked.

"Good evening, Mr Chalk. These are our new students."

The old man surveyed the group with pale, milky eyes.

"Children, this is Mr Chalk, our doorman, gardener, handyman and general caretaker. He will be making sure that you look after our academy."

"I'll be keeping a close eye on all these little hooligans," wheezed the old man.

"Now, now, Mr Chalk," said Mr Poser-Prince. "Just because they're under the age of eighteen doesn't make them hooligans."

"Hmph," muttered Mr Chalk as he swung the heavy door open. "Not in my experience."

Vip glanced up at him as he followed the others into the restaurant. He didn't like the look of Mr Chalk's pale eyes and turned away quickly. His mum and several of the children shrieked as they stepped inside. The Holly was made completely out of glass. It was like walking into an enormous greenhouse. Huge, red-spotted holly trees sprang up around the room, narrowly missing dozens of dazzling chandeliers dangling from the glass ceiling. Rows of round, mirrored tables were filled with older students all dressed in the Stardust Academy uniform, chatting with their families. The talking died down as the new arrivals trooped in. Vip couldn't bring himself to look at anyone and tucked his head into Olive, who was still draped around his neck. Mr Poser-Prince ushered them through the restaurant towards some empty tables. "Sit down, darlings," he said. "Dinner will commence after a welcoming speech from our beloved Fenella Stardust."

Vip found himself sitting next to Melody, and immediately turned bright red. She was still wearing a stripy bobble hat in addition to her uniform. His mum was on his other side chatting to Perry's mother. Perry and his puppet were next to her with Mrs Milliken and Dad opposite.

"So, what does your son do?" asked Mum. "I think I missed him at the auditions."

"Perry is a ventriloquist," she said.

Mum looked blank.

"He talks through his puppet," explained Perry's mum. "He's brilliant. You can't see his lips move at all."

Mum glanced at the mask covering the boy's mouth as Perry's mother continued talking. "I insist that he wears his surgical mask at all times," she said, "even when he's performing. You never know what's floating around in the air. I'm really worried about school dinners too. Perry is sugar, salt, dairy and anything-remotely-nice-to-eat intolerant."

"Oh dear," said Mum. "Can't he have any treats at all?"

"He's allowed to sniff chocolate every other Saturday," she answered. "I'm just hoping that becoming famous will help. Then we can have our own personal chef, dietician, dermatologist, toxicologist, homoeopath, reflexologist, hypnotherapist, acupuncturist..."

"Fame is good for everything," agreed Mum. "I myself have appeared on the cover of several newspapers and my husband is Goldwin Locks."

"Who?"

Suddenly everyone got to their feet and began clapping and cheering. Vip looked up to see Fenella Stardust slowly being lowered down from the ceiling on a glittering swing. She was wearing an all-in-one trouser suit covered in silver sequins, and a grey fur hat. Attached to the hat was a long, stripy tail, which she twirled round as she descended towards the floor. She came to rest behind a long table at the top of the room where she joined the teachers from the auditions.

"Good evening, my starlets," cried Fenella Stardust, jumping off the swing and raising her hat. "Good evening, parents. And welcome to a new year at Stardust Academy. What does fame mean?"

"Everything!" cheered the students.

Vip realized he was going to hear a lot of cheering and whooping while he was at Stardust Academy. He didn't like whooping.

"We have ten new students to welcome," announced Fenella Stardust, pointing towards their tables. "You must all get to know our first years. Networking is vital!"

Vip wasn't sure what networking was. He thought it might be something to do with fishing, and wondered why that would be so important.

"We are a small but select academy," Fenella Stardust went on, "with one class of ten students per year. All of you have been hand-picked because of your natural star quality. Here you will learn some of the most important lessons in life – how to pose for the cameras, who to be seen with, what kind of dog you should own, how to climb out of a car, and the correct etiquette when appearing on panel quiz and reality-television programmes. We also have some talent-development lessons."

"That's a relief," whispered Melody. "If I ever get to be famous, I want it to be because I'm a great musician."

Vip nodded and smiled. He was getting better at that now. He might even be able to talk to her soon.

"I, myself, have a talent for many things," said Fenella Stardust, "singing, dancing and acting to name but a few. These things are useful but not essential for becoming famous. The key thing is that everyone adores you. Hands up who adores me."

Nearly all of the hands in the room shot up. Fenella Stardust's fixed grin suddenly dropped when she noticed Vip and Melody still had their hands down.

Mum gave Vip a nudge and he slowly raised his hand, feeling very self-conscious. Melody followed. A genuine smile lit up Fenella Stardust's face and she sighed in relief. "What's not to love?" she asked. "It was my dear mother, Veronica Cheese, who first spotted my talent. As most of you know, she was a hairdresser to the stars and well known in her own right. I was brought up on TV and movie sets around the world. I was read stories and sung to by such Hollywood legends as Marilyn Money, Sylvester Gold and Sir Patrick Riches, and was inspired by their greatness – great cars and great houses. So I began performing myself, starting off in a double act and eventually going it alone. The rest, as they say, is history!"

She held up her arms and waited for the applause, grinning stupidly when it came. "I started this academy to pass on my talent," she said, "and to find the stars of the future. We have been lucky enough to have many celebrity alumni, many of whom have appeared in the wonderful magazine *Big Lips, Big Limos!*"

There were lots of gasps. Fenella Stardust nodded. "So good luck to you all during this new year. School will start formally tomorrow, but now it's time for our delicious welcoming dinner. The menu has been devised by our health and fitness instructor, Mr Robust. This term we will all be following the *Catkins Diet*. Please make sure your hands are clean before tucking in. Grubby fingers will not be tolerated. Thank you for listening and enjoy your dinner."

As the applause faded, several waiters, who Vip hadn't noticed before, jumped into action. One of them was holding a large jug of milk. But instead of filling the crystal glasses, he poured the milk into the china saucers which were set at each place.

Another waiter put a large silver platter with a domed lid on the centre of the mirrored table. He lifted the lid to reveal a huge pie. It smelled delicious. Vip inhaled deeply. The waiter took out a carving knife and cut the pie into slices.

"What type of pie is it?" asked Melody.

"It's mouse pie", replied the waiter. "This is the *Catkins Diet* – the same diet as cats and kittens. Ms Stardust has chosen it as the diet of the term, in honour of our new pet student, Olive."

"What a great idea!" cried Mum. "Does it make you thin?"

Vip's face fell as he looked at the mouse pie on the plate in front of him. He thought it probably would make him thin because he couldn't eat it. But Olive was very excited. She woke up and started purring loudly. He put the saucer of milk on the floor for her and she jumped down and lapped it up. Vip decided to eat the pastry and give the filling to Olive.

"Waiter!" called Perry Winkle's mother. "My son can't drink milk. It gives him the udder-shudders."

The waiter raised his eyebrows, but didn't question her and filled Perry's crystal glass with some water. Perry looked around to see if anyone had heard his mother and caught Vip's eye. He looked away quickly and stared into his glass, drinking the water through his mask.

To Vip's enormous relief, dinner was finished off with some ice cream.

"It's a good job cats like cream," said Melody. "The only thing I could eat was dessert."

Vip nodded again. "Me too," he managed.

Eventually all the puddings were eaten and Fenella Stardust got to her feet. The restaurant fell silent. "I hope you all enjoyed dinner," she said. "I think Mr Robust deserves a round of applause for coming up with such an ingenious diet."

There were a few unenthusiastic claps. "We all have a busy day ahead of us tomorrow," she continued. "So now it is time to say goodbye to your families and retire to your dorms for the night. There is to be no wandering about after bedtime

65

and the basement is strictly out of bounds. Finally, please remember to brush your teeth, dazzle your nails, shine your noses and vacuum your hair before going to sleep."

"Can't they just wash their hair?" asked Mrs Milliken in an extremely loud voice.

Fenella Stardust frowned and looked over at their table. Everyone else turned and stared. Melody pulled her stripy bobble hat over her face and sank down low in her chair.

"I prefer alternative methods to washing with water," said Fenella Stardust. "Water is so sloppy and wet. Vacuuming the hair removes any dust particles and reduces the risk of dull hair due to over-washing."

To Vip's dismay, Dad stood up and swished his own long, curled hair around his head. "I don't think there's any risk of *my* son having dull hair," he said. "Not with these genes."

A ripple of laughter swept around the room. Vip stared at the floor, wishing it was sinking sand. He felt a reassuring pat on his arm and looked up to see Melody peeking at him from under her hat. "Parents!" she whispered in exasperation.

Fenella Stardust stared at Vip's dad, who continued to swing his hair as if he was in a shampoo commercial.

"Erm ... if all parents would like to leave now," she said. "Then we can proceed to the dormitories and let our students settle in."

Vip's shame turned to panic. He didn't want his parents to go. They might be really embarrassing but they were still his mum and dad. "Don't leave me here," he pleaded. "I don't want to have to perform again, I hate performing. It makes me sick. And I don't know anyone."

"⬛⬛⬛⬛⬛sed said Mum, "and Olive, of course."

"I'm worried about Olive, too. I don't like the way Fenella Stardust looks at her."

"She's just a cat lover," said Dad, patting him on the back. "We have to go now, but there's nothing to worry about. And remember – if you work hard, you could end up just like me!"

67

Vip looked up at his dad's long, blonde curls, unbuttoned shirt and puffed-out chest. He sighed deeply and gave his parents a hug as Mr Chalk came into the restaurant. "Can all parents and carers please say your goodbyes and follow me?" he called.

Mum held her hand to her ear as if she were talking on a phone. "Call me," she said, blowing him a kiss. Vip watched as they joined the other families filing out of the restaurant. Melody Milliken's mother was shouting from the back of the line. "Don't forget to practise morning and night, Melody. I don't want to hear that you've been having any free time – understand?"

"Bye, Mum," called Melody.

Perry's mother had to be pr_____ ____. Make sure the pillows aren't feather, _____ cried as Mr Robust dragged her away. "The feathers could bring on a sneezing fit. And for goodness' sake, don't eat any root vegetables when it's a full moon..."

Eventually, it was just the students left in the restaurant. Fenella Stardust watched the last of the parents go, then turned and looked over the

68

children's heads directly at Olive. Vip's heart quickened. He picked Olive up and held her protectively in his lap.

"Could everyone now make their way to the dormitories," she said, walking towards Vip's table. "First years, Mr Poser-Prince will show you the way."

She circled their table, stopping when she came to Vip. "Hello, Olive."

Vip could smell her coffee breath as she reached out and tried to stroke the cat. Olive hissed and she immediately pulled her hand away and began stroking the long tail attached to her hat instead. Then she smiled and turned on her heels, striding out of The Holly without another word.

Vip clung to Olive and tried to ignore the dark thoughts battering his brain. Why did Fenella Stardust want Olive so badly? And how was he going to cope in a school like this?

6

Nail-Dazzlers, Hair-Vacuumers and Nose-shiners

Mr Poser-Prince did a quick headcount before leading the class out of a back door and into an enormous circular courtyard. In the centre was a stone fountain. Jets of water in rainbow shades sprayed from the upturned fingertips of a huge statue of Fenella Stardust. Parked around the edge of the courtyard were fifteen small silver caravans. Each of them was lit up by a set of different coloured spotlights.

"These are the academy dormitories," said Mr Poser-Prince. "There will be three or four of you in each trailer."

Vip stared at the caravans. They were tiny. It was going to be a bit of a squeeze.

"Melody Milliken, Pineapple Bunting and Cherry Dropp are in the indigo trailer," continued Mr Poser-Prince. "Miss Maykova will be along shortly, girls, to help you unpack."

"YEEEESSSS!!!" screamed Cherry Dropp. "We're roomies, we're roomies, we're roomies. We're going to be best friends for ever! This is going to be UNBELIEVABLISTIC!"

Vip felt a stab of panic as Cherry dragged Melody into a lilac-blue caravan. She was the only person he could talk to – and he could barely even talk to her. Reluctantly he followed Mr Poser-Prince towards a trailer lit up by a set of shocking-pink lights. "In the magenta trailer, we have Dwayne Pipes, Perry Winkle and Vip Locks," said Mr Poser-Prince, checking his clipboard.

Vip glanced nervously at his new room-mates. Dwayne grinned at him but Perry eyed them both suspiciously over his surgical mask. As they stepped inside, Perry's puppet squeaked in surprise,

71

Dwayne let out a long whistle and Vip's mouth fell open. The interior was huge – far bigger than the caravan itself. It was separated into four different areas. Three of the corners had enormous pink wardrobes, matching beds and long dressing tables. Above the tables were mirrors framed with bright light bulbs. The fourth corner was taken up by a pink sofa that curved around two walls with a glass coffee table in front. On the wall above the sofa was a framed signed photograph of Fenella Stardust, and hanging from the centre of the ceiling and revolving slowly was a large glitter ball. Drops of light reflected from the mirrors and raced around the walls making Vip feel dizzy. There was a second door at the far end which led to a bathroom.

Mr Poser-Prince popped his head through the front door. "You'll find your nail-dazzlers, hair-vacuumers and nose-shiners along with an instruction manual in the drawer under the sofa," he said. "They're all very simple to operate, so make sure you use them. In the bathroom is a tube of our school toothpaste, Whitening-Bolt. Please do not use any other brands.

I'll leave you to get to know each other now, but someone will be along later to make sure you've got everything you need. Once you're in your trailers for the night there is to be no walking around the rest of the school – OK? Breakfast will be served at half past eight tomorrow morning in The Holly. Don't be late. Goodnight, boys."

The metal door closed with a clank. Vip looked around the room. He watched as Dwayne jumped on to one of the big beds and bounced right off. Perry inspected his bedding distrustfully before propping his puppet up on a fluffy pink pillow.

"How come we get the magenta trailer?" grumbled the puppet in a gruff voice. "We're pink intolerant!"

Vip stared at Perry's puppet. It was as if it had talked by itself. Perry himself was busy unpacking. Suddenly, Dwayne broke out into song.

"Pink is the colour of roses," he sang, *"pink is the colour of love."*

His voice was extremely deep and loud for such a tiny boy.

"Pink is the colour of angels, sent from the heavens above."

Vip kept his head down and made his way to the free corner bedroom. He didn't want to get to know his new room-mates; he didn't want to be there at all. He managed to unpack without looking or speaking to them, then sat down on his bed and cuddled Olive. He could hear Perry and his puppet whispering to each other. Dwayne was still singing loudly. *"Nessun dorma, nessun dorma. . ."*

Vip tried to fix his attention on Olive, but she jumped down from his lap and sauntered over to Perry and his puppet. Perry looked as uncomfortable as Vip felt. He tried to shoo Olive away but she seemed very determined to sniff the puppet.

"Excuse me," said Perry. "Your cat won't leave us alone."

Olive was sitting on Perry's bed next to the puppet.

"Olive, come here," called Vip.

She came strolling back to him, purring loudly. Perry tightened his mask and began frantically brushing the spot she had sat on.

"I'm allergic to cats," he muttered, grabbing his puppet and dusting it off.

"Sorry," said Vip quietly. "What happens if you touch one?"

"I don't know," answered Perry, "I've never touched one before."

"So how do you know you're allergic?"

"My mum said I was . . . might be. . ."

There was an awkward silence before Dwayne suddenly broke out into song again. *"Maybe you are, maybe you're not, Maybe you'll sneeze and get covered in sn—"*

"Maybe it's time to check out the nail-dazzlers and hair-vacuumers," interrupted Perry, "and what was the other thing?"

"Nose-shiners," added Vip.

They all left their corners and gathered in the lounge area. Perry looked under the sofa and pulled out a large drawer. He lifted out a thin instruction booklet and three small feather dusters on sticks.

"These are our nose-shiners," he said. "According to this book they are ten times more efficient than cleaning with water. They're battery operated and rotate one hundred times per minute."

Vip examined his nose-shiner cautiously.

"Step one," read Perry from the book. "Press the feather buffer gently against the tip of your nose. Step two, push the red button. Step three, hold for twenty-two seconds."

Vip did as he was told and switched on the nose-shiner. It was very tickly and he couldn't help giggling. Perry had poked his nose-shiner inside his mask and was chuckling too, and Dwayne was laughing so much, he had to dash to the toilet halfway through.

When Dwayne returned they all studied each other's noses. Their skin certainly looked healthy and glowing. Dwayne's nose was so shiny Vip could almost see his reflection in it. Next Perry lifted three pairs of yellow washing-up gloves out of the drawer.

"These must be the nail-dazzlers," he said, looking at the instruction manual. "We have to put them on, wave our hands in the air and shout 'razzle-dazzle' at the top of our voices."

Vip followed the instructions, feeling very stupid. But the moment he shouted "razzle-dazzle", he felt a strange tingling sensation running through his fingertips from the knuckle to the nail, followed by a loud pop.

"When your fingernails have popped," read Perry, "you can remove the gloves."

Vip took his rubber gloves off and looked at his hands. They were gleaming, and his fingernails had never been so clean. He turned at the sound of a small scream beside him. Dwayne was staring in horror at his own nails. They were bright pink.

"Oh dear," said Perry, flicking through the booklet. "It doesn't say anything in here about painted nails. Those gloves must be faulty, Dwayne. Mr Poser-Prince said someone will be along later to see if we're OK. I'm sure they'll find some nail-varnish remover for you. In the meantime, let's move on to the hair-vacuumers to take your mind off it."

Dwayne tucked his fingers in his pockets and nodded as Perry unpacked three glass helmets with hoses attached to bags. Vip noticed that each bag was labelled with their name.

"I guess these are the hair-vacuumers," said Perry. "We have to put them on – make sure you take the one with your name on – and press the switch at the side."

Vip wondered why the bags had to be labelled. He lowered the helmet down over his head and glanced anxiously at Perry and Dwayne. They all looked as if they were about to take a walk on the moon.

"It says here to take a deep breath before turning on," continued Perry.

Vip closed his eyes and pressed the button. A loud drone filled his ears and he gasped in surprise as his hair was whipped up like a palm tree in a hurricane. After the initial shock, it was actually quite calming. He looked over at the other two. Perry's hair was so long when it was sucked straight that it filled his whole helmet, hiding his face. Vip could just make out his mask flying around inside. Dwayne seemed to have forgotten all about his pink nails and was obviously enjoying the whole experience enormously. His mouth was wide open and although Vip couldn't hear anything above the noise of the vacuumer, he guessed that Dwayne was singing loudly.

After a minute the vacuumers stopped automatically. Vip pulled the helmet off. His hair was so fine that it immediately settled back into its natural position. But Perry's fanned out around his head like a huge, hairy peacock, and Dwayne looked like a singing hedgehog. *"At first it was quite scary,"* he warbled, *"as I'm really not that hairy. But the vacuuming sensation, was a pleasing revelation."*

A loud knock on the door made everyone jump. They all turned around as Fenella Stardust poked her head in, her fur hat rippling gently in the evening breeze.

7

Hair bags

The boys' trailer was immediately filled with the smell of Fenella Stardust's coffee breath and a whiff of something else – something slightly carroty.

"Good evening, my starlets," she said. "How's everyone settling in?"

"Ms Stardust!" cried Perry. "We didn't realize it would be you who was coming to see us."

"I like to make sure that all our new arrivals have everything they need, Perry," she said, smiling broadly. "Have you got to grips with all the cleaning equipment?"

Dwayne held up his pink nails and started singing.

"I'm such a fan, Ms Stardust,
And you know I'll try my hardest,
But I'm feeling kind of surly,
'Cause my nails have gone all girly."

"Oh, Dwayne, you poor thing," said Fenella Stardust. "You must have got a pair of the fifth year girls' gloves by accident. If you go and see Miss Maykova in the morning, she'll have some nail-varnish remover that you can borrow. And I'll get Mr Chalk to replace the gloves with a more suitable pair. Happy?"

Dwayne began bouncing on his bed again. *"I'm happy, I'm happy, I'm totally dappy,"* he sang. *"I feel so excited, I might need a nappy."*

"Let's hope that won't be necessary, but it's wonderful to see such enthusiasm."

Fenella Stardust looked around the trailer. Her eyes settled on Vip's corner of the room.

"Where's Olive?" she asked, completely ignoring Vip.

He glanced at the floor. He could see Olive's tail

poking out from under his bed. Perry followed his gaze to where Olive was hiding. She was shaking.

Perry stepped forward, clutching his puppet. Its painted mouth slowly opened. "I think the cat might have gone out for a night-time stroll, Ms Stardust," said the doll in the same gruff voice.

"Oh dear," muttered Fenella Stardust. "I really wanted to see her. Are you sure?"

She stopped and turned to face Perry, staring right into his puppet's brown eyes. "Hold on a minute," she said.

Vip thought he heard the puppet gulp.

"I can't believe I'm talking to a puppet. Amazing, Perry! I didn't see your lips move at all."

"That's because he's wearing a mask," replied the puppet.

Fenella Stardust began snorting like an overexcited pig. It took Vip a minute to realize that she was laughing.

"Well, I don't think having a surgical mask is a bad thing," she chortled. "I might even get one for myself to protect me from all that nasty dust out there.

Speaking of which, your noses all look wonderfully clean. Remember to keep on using the nose-shiners instead of washing your faces with water."

"What's wrong with water?" asked Perry.

The ends of Fenella Stardust's mouth turned down. "Nasty, soggy stuff," she said. "The nose-shiners are far more efficient at cleaning, as are the hair-vacuumers. I'm afraid I haven't got one to fit your puppet, Perry, but I am designing one for cats. Isn't that exciting?"

Vip glanced down at Olive again. There was no way he was going to let her be vacuumed.

"Perry and Dwayne, I would like you to vacuum your hair every other day," she continued, "but feel free to use them anytime. And you..." She trailed off as she looked at Vip for the first time. "Sorry, what's your name again?"

"Vip."

"Skip?"

"No, Vi—"

"Yes, whatever ... as long as you keep yourself clean and tidy ... but it's really Olive who will

83

benefit the most from this whole process. Anyway, boys, when you've finished vacuuming your hair, just pop the waste bags that are attached to the hoses in this rubbish chute and they will be collected from outside every Monday night."

She pulled the bags off the vacuumers and posted them through a letter box in the wall.

"What happens to the bags?" asked Perry.

"Oh, they're just full of dust," answered Fenella Stardust. "They get destroyed."

"So why do you label them, then?" said Vip.

Fenella Stardust stopped in her tracks and stared at him. "You're gaining in confidence," she said. "Good! Nice to see you're taking an interest in the hair-vacuumers ... and soon we shall be able to vacuum Olive too."

Olive was still crouched under Vip's bed. "You can't vacuum my cat," he said. "She won't like it."

Fenella Stardust's taut face suddenly turned a nasty shade of orange and her eyebrows tugged at her rigid forehead in an attempt to frown. "I can vacuum whoever or whatever I want," she snapped, her smile replaced with a horrible scowl. "Remember, you are only here because of that cat!"

She stopped abruptly, then slowly the set smile returned to her face. "Please don't make me cross – frown lines can cause wrinkles. Now, it's time for me to go, my starlets, and time for you to get some beauty sleep. Your first lesson tomorrow is with Mr Robust, so you need to be dressed in your PE kits. Sleep well. Goodnight."

She swept out of the door with a final wave. Perry closed it after her.

"Blimey!" he said. "I can't believe you talked back to Fenella Stardust. I thought you were quiet."

"I'm just looking out for my cat," murmured Vip.

"*Hey diddle diddle,*" sang Dwayne, "*the cat and the . . . vacuum cleaner. . .*"

"That's not funny, Dwayne," said Perry, "and technically incorrect."

Vip couldn't help smiling. He knelt down and coaxed Olive out from under the bed. "Thank you," he said, "for saying Olive had gone out."

"I didn't. It was Conker," answered Perry, holding up his puppet.

"Conker?" repeated Vip.

Perry covered the puppet's ears with his hands. "He's called that because he's made out of a conker tree," he whispered. "But don't mention that he's made from wood. He's very sensitive about it. Apparently, lots of puppets are."

"R-right," said Vip. He glanced over at Dwayne, who was nodding solemnly and pretending to zip up his mouth. Perry uncovered his puppet's ears.

"Conker can be a bit suspicious of new people, but I think he likes Olive, don't you, Conker?"

The puppet nodded its little wooden head as Perry continued talking. "Fenella Stardust seems very keen on your cat too, but for some reason, I don't think Olive likes her very much. Conker could see Olive's tail shaking and he felt sorry for her. That's why he did it. But he feels completely conked out now – and so do I. We should all try and get some sleep. It's our first full day tomorrow, and Dwayne's got to get up early and find Miss Maykova before anyone sees his nails."

Dwayne nodded and disappeared into the bathroom again. Vip was feeling very tired too. He pulled on his pyjamas, climbed into bed and turned out his bedside lamp. Olive curled up on his pillow. He lay on his back, staring up at the glitter ball. It was strange sharing a room with other people, especially when one communicated through song, and the other seemed to think his puppet had feelings. But at least they stood up for Olive. Maybe his room-mates weren't that bad after all.

8

The Personal Trainers

Vip was woken up the next day by Dwayne singing in the bathroom. *"Good morning, eyes, good morning, nose, good morning, teeth, good morning, toes."*

Vip rubbed his eyes. He'd been having a horrible dream about the hair-vacuumers. He dreamt that his whole body had been sucked down the hose into a labelled bag and delivered to Fenella Stardust.

He sat up and looked around him. Olive was sitting on Perry's knee, with Conker on the other knee.

"Why do cats always jump on people who either don't like them or are allergic to them?" asked Perry. "Are you feeling sneezy, Conker?"

The puppet shook its head.

"Hmm . . . me neither," continued Perry. "Maybe I could take my mask off. . ."

"Morning," said Vip. "I'm afraid Olive seems to like you."

"She and Conker have become quite close," said Perry. "We've been up for ages. And Dwayne has already been to see Miss Maykova. You'd better get ready. It's past eight o'clock and we need to get down to The Holly for breakfast. Conker and I have got our PE kits on already."

Perry and his puppet were both dressed in gold t-shirts and matching silver shorts. They had pink sweatbands wrapped around their heads, flattening their springy hair. Olive came wandering over when she saw that Vip was awake. He picked her up and gave her a quick stroke before opening his new wardrobe and searching for the PE kit he had stuffed in there the night before. He grabbed the shiny clothes and walked towards the bathroom just as Dwayne emerged smelling of lavender soap. *"Good morning, wwwwwworld!"*

Vip smiled politely and closed the bathroom door behind him. He pulled on his PE kit and quickly brushed his teeth with the Whitening-Bolt toothpaste. Immediately his teeth began to glow. He stared at his reflection in the mirror. It looked like he'd swallowed a light bulb, but then gradually his teeth began to fade. Eventually they returned to a shade slightly lighter than their original colour.

Dwayne and Perry were waiting for him when he walked out. He put Olive on his shoulder and followed them out of the trailer, across the courtyard and back into The Holly. The top table where the teachers had sat the night before was now filled with a buffet-style breakfast. Queues of students lined up to fill their plates. Vip saw Melody already eating at one of the tables. She smiled and waved at him. He lifted his hand and gave a tiny flick, feeling very pleased with himself. Breakfast consisted of kippers and cat biscuits. Olive was very happy. Vip sat between Perry and Dwayne.

"We've got PE all morning with Mr Robust," said Perry. "Apparently he's an ex-army officer – an

American Marine! It's going to be hard work. Eat up your breakfast, we're going to need lots of energy. I hope these cat biscuits are gluten-free."

Vip smiled. Perry was a bit of a fusspot, but a nice fusspot. Suddenly the doors to The Holly were flung open and Mr Robust sprinted into the restaurant. He stood in the middle of the room with his hands on his hips. His black hair was cropped short, and his dark skin shone as if it were polished. He rolled up the sleeves of his silver tracksuit and looked around the tables. "ATTENNNNNNNTION!" he bellowed.

Everyone jumped to their feet.

"All first years stand in line behind me by the count of three – ONE!"

Vip dropped his knife and fork on top of his half-eaten kipper.

"TWO!"

He ran to the centre of the room and desperately tried to squeeze into line behind the rest of the panicking first years.

"THREE!"

Vip stood rigidly to attention.

"Not bad," said Mr Robust, walking down the line and inspecting everyone. "You will proceed to the gym in an orderly line behind me. Left, right, left, right!"

They all marched out of The Holly behind Mr Robust. "Repeat after me," he shouted. *I don't know but it's been said.*

"I don't know but it's been said," repeated the children.

"Fame can make you lose your head."
"Fame can make you lose your head."

"We don't care, we want the thrill."
"We don't care we want the thrill."

"Even if it makes us ill."
"Even if it makes us ill."

They marched and sang along the corridors until they came to an enormous gymnasium. Standing in the centre of the room was a large vaulting box and a balance beam surrounded by soft mats. A tall climbing frame took up an entire wall, and running machines and fitness bikes lined up along another. At the far end, thick ropes dangled from the ceiling to the floor. Mr Chalk, the caretaker, emerged from a side door and shuffled across the hall towards them. "Ah, Mr Robust," he said. "I've left the *personal trainers* in the changing room, as requested."

"Thank you, Mr Chalk."

Vip glanced nervously towards the changing rooms. He wasn't very sporty, and now as well as Mr Robust barking orders, he was going to have his own personal trainer. It was going from bad to worse. Mr Chalk walked past the class before stopping to look them up and down. "You're going to need all the help you can get with this lot, Mr Robust," he muttered.

"I sure am," replied Mr Robust. "But I am a great believer in PMA, Mr Chalk. P-M-A – Positive Mental Attitude!"

"Hmm, I'm sure you are," sniffed Mr Chalk, opening the door to leave. "Don't go messing up my clean floor with your PMA. I've been polishing it all over the summer holidays."

Mr Robust turned to face the class as Mr Chalk left the gym. "I am here to prepare you for fame," he yelled. "I need to get you into shape physically and mentally. We are going to warm up by running around the gym shouting – *No dream is too extreme*! Got it?"

Everyone nodded uncertainly as Mr Robust began sprinting round the gym. "Let's go, hotshots!" he shouted. "No dream is too extreme! Let me hear you say it."

The whole class took off in different directions. Vip had no choice but to join in. He felt too self-conscious to chant anything, so he just mouthed the words, hoping that Mr Robust wouldn't notice. Olive clung to his shoulders as he jogged past Dwayne, who was singing the wrong song. "*I'm dreaming of butterflies and rainbows. . .*"

After several minutes of Mr Robust shouting "louder" and "faster" and "get those knees higher", they were allowed to slow down and eventually stop. Vip sank down on to one of the mats, panting heavily. He had a painful stitch. Perry flopped beside him. His glasses had steamed up and Vip could see that behind his mask, his skin was shiny with exertion. However, all the panting and puffing seemed to be coming from Conker.

"That was unacceptable!" shouted Mr Robust. "Where was the speed? Where was the pace? Where was the P-M-A?" He walked towards the changing rooms. "I think it's time for the personal trainers."

Mr Robust disappeared into the changing room and came back carrying a small box. Vip looked around expecting to see more fitness instructors, but Mr Robust seemed to be alone. He opened the box. Inside were ten tiny pairs of training shoes. "These are your personal trainers," he said, holding up a small shoe for everyone to see.

"They're teensy," said Perry. "Perfect for Conker, but—"

"Come here, Pinocchio," shouted Mr Robust, beckoning Perry and his puppet over.

"His name's not Pinocchio, it's Conk—"

"Closer," said Mr Robust, reaching out his thick arm towards Perry's curly hair. He grabbed hold of a couple of strands and yanked.

"OUCH!"

"Settle down, soldier," said Mr Robust, "and watch."

He pulled back the insoles of a pair of shoes and placed a strand of hair inside each one. Immediately the trainers began to change colour from bright white to a soft mellow-brown. And at the same time, they began to grow; but not only in length. Towards the back of the heel they started sprouting dark, curly hair, and the laces curved around to form a pair of thick glasses. Vip couldn't believe what he was seeing. The trainers looked just like Perry.

"Here," said Mr Robust, handing Perry the shoes. "Try them on. They are now infused with your personal DNA – a little bit of you, in your shoe. Not only will they be the perfect fit, but they are programmed with a precise exercise regime just for you."

Vip watched as Perry put on the personal trainers. He then sprinted across the gym, dragging Conker behind him, jumped on to a cycling machine and began peddling furiously. Mr Robust nodded in approval. "OK, everybody," he said. "Take a pair of trainers and place a strand of your hair inside each shoe."

Vip did as he was told, then looked on in amazement as his trainers turned a pale pinky-tan and developed mousy-brown hair and freckles. He was just about to put them on when Dwayne marched past him. The laces of his trainers were parted perfectly and the tongues were poking out and singing loudly.

> *"If you want to get fit, use a Personal Trainer,*
> *No extra kit, it is such a no-brainer."*

Vip looked around him. The whole class had sprung into action. Melody was halfway up a climbing rope. The laces on her trainers were pulled back like strings on a violin. They were attached to four tuning pegs that poked out from the heels. Cherry Dropp's trainers were jumping up and down, screaming excitedly, and Merlin McGandalf was flying through the air and over the vaulting box in the centre of the room. Vip was sure he could see a pair of small broomsticks attached to the sides of his trainers. Pineapple Bunting, the ballet dancer, pirouetted past, her blonde laces scraped back into two neat buns at the back of her heels. Vip took a deep breath and looked down at his own trainers. Apart from the scruffy brown hair and dotty freckles they didn't really stand out at all. Olive climbed down from his shoulders and sniffed the shoes as Mr Robust approached them.

"You're the guy who tried to run away from the auditions," he said. "What's your name, soldier?"

"V-vip," he whispered.

"Zip?"

"N-no ... Vi—"

"Your trainers don't look very dynamic, Zip," said Mr Robust looking disdainfully down at Vip's mousy shoes. "But I don't see mediocrity as a problem, I see it as a challenge."

Vip wasn't too sure what mediocrity meant, but he didn't want to be a problem or a challenge. He just wanted to be left alone.

"However," Mr Robust continued, "I'm more concerned about your cat right now. Ms Stardust has specifically requested that Olive has her own personal trainers."

Mr Robust held up two pairs of tiny shoes. But as soon as he came near, Olive ran across the gym and jumped out of an open window. Mr Robust huffed angrily. "I've got as much chance of getting shoes on a cat as I have of feeling negative," he muttered.

Vip was glad that Olive had managed to escape. She would come and find him later. Mr Robust beckoned Vip closer but his trainers had other ideas. They immediately took off on their own accord and scurried to a corner of the room. The moment anyone came near him they blushed and ran away at a tremendous rate, leaving him breathless. Mr Robust eventually gave up and continued jogging around the gym chanting, "no dream is too extreme", and other motivational quotes. Everyone looked completely out of control. Melody came jogging towards him. "How are you getting on?" she panted.

Vip opened his mouth and tried to answer but his trainers turned a deep shade of scarlet and shot up the huge climbing frame. He looked down at the small figure of Melody far below him.

"Mine keep practising the same thing over and over again," she called up. "And they don't stop until it's perfect. I'm exhausted!"

She wasn't the only one. A boy with short fair hair dashed past looking terrified. His trainers were yodelling loudly, the long tongues flapping furiously.

"That's Gunter Gruber," cried Melody. "And look at poor Ben Dee!"

A tall skinny boy was coiled into a tight ball and was bouncing around the gym like a crazed basketball. Vip watched from the top of the climbing frame as his whole class dashed frantically about. He suddenly remembered what his mum had said about magic being used at Stardust Academy. Vip didn't think he believed in magic but now he wasn't quite so sure.

The PE lesson seemed to go on for ever, but eventually Mr Robust managed to round them all up and allowed everyone to take off their personal trainers. They staggered back to The Holly for a lunch of *salmon a la kitty*. Vip sat at a table with Melody, Perry and Dwayne.

"That was unbelievable," said Perry. "I'd heard rumours about the unusual lessons here but I wasn't expecting that. I'm exhausted! All that exercise could give me athlete's foot."

"What's that?" asked Melody.

"I don't know," answered Perry. "I've never had it but my mum..." He stopped and thought for a moment. "Who are you, anyway?"

"Oh, sorry," said Vip. "This is ... um ... erm..." He could feel his face getting hotter. "M-Melody Milliken."

Perry grinned at her. "I remember you from the auditions. You were good."

"Thanks, I remember you too," said Melody. "I couldn't see your mouth move at all."

Perry reached up and touched his surgical mask.

"Conker thinks I should take my mask off."

"Who's Conker?"

Perry held up his puppet.

"Oh, I can see why he's called that," said Melody. "He's a lovely colour. Is he made from a horse-chestnut tree?"

Perry gasped and Dwayne and Vip both grimaced as Conker's little wooden mouth fell open.

"WHAT DID SHE SAY?" yelled the puppet in his deep, gravelly voice.

Melody's eyes swivelled uncertainly from the puppet to Perry.

"She said she owns a horse," said Perry, "who is the colour of a chestnut tree..."

The puppet made a little huffing noise. Vip could have sworn he was sulking.

"Sorry," said Melody. "I didn't mean any offence."

"Don't worry, he's just a bit sensitive," answered Perry. "Anyway, I was just saying that Conker thinks I should take my mask off. But I don't know. My mum says to keep it on at all times, just in case."

"In case of what?" asked Melody.

"Allergies, allergies, gross abnormalities," piped up Dwayne. "Got to be careful in case of fatalities."

"Exactly," agreed Perry. He was about to elaborate when Fenella Stardust came sweeping into The Holly. Her stripy fur hat not only had a tail, but ears as well. Olive jumped down from Vip's shoulder and dived under the table.

"Could I please have everyone's attention," she shouted. "I'm sorry to interrupt your lunch but I've got some very exciting news. I have just heard that at the end of this term, I will be hosting my very own Christmas-special TV show. *Fenella Stardust's Showbiz Extravaganza – Live!*"

Everyone apart from Vip started clapping. He was beginning to feel very uneasy.

"And it won't just be me on that stage," continued Fenella Stardust. "Two of Stardust Academy's finest graduates will also be there. Chardonnay Frontage will be promoting her latest autobiography, detailing the time she spent in her mother's womb, and Steven Stolid will be there sucking his toes!"

There were several gasps and "wows" from

around the room. "But the best part is – I will be picking several students to perform alongside me."

The word "perform" struck terror in Vip's heart. He knew how much Fenella Stardust liked Olive. What if they were forced to take part? He hated getting up in front of *one* person – but a Christmas TV show? That would mean millions.

9

Personal Image

After lunch it was time for Personal Image class in the academy's beauty salon. Everyone except for Vip was still buzzing with excitement at the thought of appearing on a live TV show. He was finding it hard to concentrate as they lined up outside a red door. Miss Maykova opened it and beckoned them in with long, crimson nails. She was very tall. Her thick blonde hair was tied into a large bun on top of her head and she was wearing a scarlet suit. Vip cringed, remembering the time he was sick on her lap. She peered down at him and pursed her massive lips.

"Ah, ze boy wiz ze cat," she said, looking past him

at Olive. "Ms Stardust has specifically requested zat Olive's coat is not to be touched. Shame. I think she would look great wiz a pink tail."

She ushered them all inside. "Velcome to Stardust Academy's very own beauty salon," she said with a smile that took up two thirds of her face.

There were several excited gasps from the class. Vip looked around him. All the desks had their own mirrors, sinks, hairdryers and brushes. One wall was lined with shelves from floor to ceiling, packed full of brightly coloured bottles and jars. He could just make out the label on a particularly large urn – *Lard-Loaded Lip Filler*.

"A beauty salon for a beauty queen," continued Miss Maykova, "I am ze former Miss Latvionia – and my job is to make you physically perfect."

She surveyed them all with large blue eyes. Vip could feel a slight breeze every time she blinked her enormous false eyelashes. "Is there anybody here who is happy wiz ze way zey look?"

Most of the class looked embarrassed by the question, but Dwayne nodded his head and smiled.

Miss Maykova pointed a long red finger at him. "Vell, you shouldn't be!" she barked. "You are too short!"

The smile on Dwayne's face dropped suddenly.

"Imperfections are not tolerated in ze fame game," she continued. "But do not vorry. Ve have a stretching machine for ze short ones." Dwayne swallowed loudly. "And squashing machines for ze tall ones. Ve also have nose-squishers, ear-flatteners, cheekbone-sharpeners and pimple-poppers for ven you become spotty teenagers. Ve have hair dyes, eye dyes, teeth dyes, nail dyes and tongue dyes. But today ve vill be focusing on ze hair." She beckoned Melody over with a long talon.

"Take off zat dreadful hat," she said. Melody did as she was told. "You have nice red hair, but maybe ve should spot it wiz gold paint?"

"Maybe..." murmured Melody, "but I don't think that's going to help my violin playing..."

"Nonsense!" snapped Miss Maykova. "Of course it vill! People vont glamour, glamour and more glam— oh my goodness! Vot is zat?"

She had turned her attention to Perry. "Vot is zat on your head?"

"My surgical mask?" he asked. "You can't be too careful when it comes to wafting wheat—"

"Not ze mask," she cried, "I'm talking about zat tangle around your head!"

"Erm . . . my hair?"

"Curly-curly is a no-no at ze moment. It is *so* last season! Ve need it straight-straight. Follow me."

She led Perry into a booth at the side of the room. He was clutching Conker who was looking around anxiously. "Everyone gather round and votch," she said. "Give ze poopet to me."

"I am not a *poopet*!" stated Conker in his surliest voice.

"And he never leaves my side," added Perry.

"Very vell, you may hold on to your dolly. Lie face down on ze table." She pointed to what looked like a big ironing board with a hole at one end. Perry lay down on his stomach with his face through the hole. His arms were wrapped around the ironing board holding Conker underneath.

Miss Maykova poured some water into a large iron and a huge cloud of steam engulfed them. "I vill now iron ze hair, taking care not to burn ze scalp."

She pulled clumps of Perry's hair flat against the table and proceeded to iron it straight. When she had finished she did exactly the same to Conker.

"All done," she said. "Even ze poopet looks much better."

Vip stared at Perry. His hair was now parted in the middle and hung straight down, right past his shoulders.

"The poopet prefers curly-curly," muttered Conker.

Vip couldn't help laughing.

"Get into pairs," said Miss Maykova. "Sit at one of ze desks and see if you can improve your partner's hair."

Before Vip had a chance to think about it, Melody had grabbed him and sat him down in front of a mirror.

"OK, has everybody got a partner?" asked Miss

Maykova. "Dwayne is with Merlin, Cherry with Perry, Ben with Gunter, Pineapple with Howl and Melody with . . . Pip?"

"His name is Vip," said Melody.

"You have your work cut out wiz zis boy, my dear," she said to Melody. "He is unbelievably plain. I think you might be vasting your time."

"I don't think I'm wasting my time," replied Melody. She leaned closer to Vip and whispered, "I'd rather be plain than look like Miss Lardy-Lips."

Miss Maykova shrugged her shoulders and moved on to the next desk where Cherry was attempting to tie Perry's hair up in bunches. "I'm going to make you look gorgeoulicious," she squealed.

Vip glanced over at Perry's panic-stricken face and then back at Melody. They both giggled.

"Poor Perry," she whispered.

Vip smiled and nodded.

"You're not much of a talker, are you?" said Melody.

"I . . . erm . . . not really."

"That's OK," she said, rifling through a drawer

in front of them and pulling out a pot of gel. "I like talking. I've wanted to speak to you for ages."

"Oh . . . um . . ."

"We live near each other."

Vip wanted to say, *I know, I've seen you lots of times,* but he could only manage another smile. Melody dipped her hand in the pot of gel.

"I can't see the point in all this image nonsense," she said, rubbing her hands together, "but if I'm going to do something, I like to do it well."

Vip watched in the mirror as she began to spike up the front of his hair. He felt he had to say something. It would be rude not to. He breathed in.

"I-is that why you're here?" he asked. "I mean . . . at the academy."

Melody smiled. "I'm here because I want to be a brilliant violinist. If I'm the best in the world then that might make me famous. But I don't want to be famous just for the sake of it. I don't want to be followed around by gangs of photographers and have everything I do in the papers. My mum would like that. She wants me to be a superstar. I'm happy to be here, though. I can cope with all these silly classes as long as I get to play the violin. I'm having private lessons with Miss Stradivarius. She's the best in the country."

"That's great," said Vip, feeling a bit more confident.

"Yep. But that's not the only reason I want to be here. I need to get away from my mum. I love her, but I think a boarding school might give me a bit of freedom – let me make some choices of my own for a change. What about you?"

"M-me?"

"Yes."

"Erm ... well to be honest, I don't want to be famous at all," said Vip. "I want to be ... a vet."

He stopped suddenly, worried that he'd said too much and Melody would laugh at him.

"A vet?" she repeated.

"Well ... I ... um..."

"Now that *is* cool."

"Really?"

"Yes, really."

Vip felt his ears go pink and hoped that Melody didn't notice. He was enjoying talking to her. It was really quite easy once he got going.

"So why are you here at Stardust Academy, then?" she asked.

"It wasn't me Fenella Stardust wanted, it was Olive. And now I'm really worried that she might pick Olive to appear on this TV show, because that will mean I'll have to do it too."

"Can't you tell your parents you don't want to be here?"

"They won't listen. They're desperate for me to be famous. They want me to live up to my name and become a V-I-P."

"I'm sure you're already very important to them."

"Don't be too sure," he sighed.

"My mum is pretty pushy too," said Melody. "Her favourite saying is, 'We Milliken girls can do anything!' She thinks that I should practise the violin every second of every day. She's even more

113

of a perfectionist than me. I've tried to tell her that I play better when I've had a few breaks but she won't listen. She never listens. . ."

Melody paused before carrying on chatting about music. She asked what songs Vip liked as she did his hair. She was easy to talk to because she did most of the talking. He liked that.

"There you go," she said after a few minutes. "What do you think?"

She had gelled his hair into a small quiff. It actually looked quite good. "Thanks," he said, getting out of the chair. "Do you want gold paint on yours?"

"Not really, but if it keeps Miss Lardy-Lips happy, then maybe I should. Besides, the hair-vacuumers will get rid of anything we do to our hair today."

"That's another thing I'm worried about," said Vip, picking up the gold spray-paint. "Don't you think it's a bit strange, having to vacuum our hair all the time?"

"Fenella Stardust is obsessed with cleanliness," answered Melody. "She hates dirt and dust."

"I know, but why are the hair bags labelled with our names?"

"That's just the way she does things. The hair bags go down the waste chute and are collected from the outside every Monday night."

"We were told that too, but collected for what? It's . . . weird."

"So is polishing your nose, dazzling your nails and eating cat food, but we have to do that. Why are you so interested in the hair bags, anyway?"

Vip felt embarrassed again. "I'm not. It's just. . ."

"What?"

"Erm . . . nothing."

"Tell me."

He looked around to make sure no one else was listening. "It's just . . . I don't really trust Fenella Stardust . . . she smells of carrots."

Melody giggled. "I think that's the smell of her fake tan, and that's no reason to dislike her."

Vip shrugged. "Anyway, *she* doesn't like *me*."

"Ah, so that's what this is all about."

"No! I don't care if she doesn't like me. I prefer it

when she ignores me . . . but something's not right. Why would she label bags of dirt if they're going to be destroyed? It doesn't make sense."

"OK, so what are you going to do about it?"

"N-nothing."

"I never do nothing," said Melody.

She was quiet for a moment before speaking again. "Look, I'm sure the bags end up in the rubbish. But if it makes you feel better, we could hide outside on collection day and see what happens to them."

Vip stopped squirting the gold spray-paint. "It's collection day today," he whispered.

Melody's eyes flashed and a small smile lit up her face. "I know!"

"I'm not sure if that's a good idea. We could get into trouble."

"I know!" she repeated. "I've never been in trouble in my life. I've never had time. My mum would go mad."

"We'd better not do it, then—"

"No! We have to do it. I could meet you by the

fountain tonight after hair-vacuuming. What do you think?"

Vip hesitated.

"You're scared," she sighed.

"No, I'm not," he whispered. "OK – tonight."

10

The Basement

That evening, Vip couldn't concentrate on his sparrow spaghetti. He ate the pasta and gave the sauce to Olive, then wandered back to the dormitories with Perry.

"If you think my hair's bad," said Perry as they approached their trailer, "you should see Dwayne's. He was paired up with Merlin for the hairdressing. Apparently Merlin just tapped Dwayne's head with a wand and—"

The door of their trailer opened revealing a stunned-looking Dwayne. His normally neatly parted hair was standing on end. It was luminous green and small fireworks were shooting out of the tips.

"Miss Maykova gave Merlin a merit for good work," continued Perry. "It's not fair, if you ask me. Come on, Dwayne. Let's get the hair-vacuumers on. I think we all need it tonight."

They put on their glass helmets and pressed the buttons. Dwayne was soon singing again and everyone was pleased to get rid of their strange hairstyles. Vip noticed that as Perry's hair sprang back into place, so did Conker's, even though he didn't fit into the hair-vacuumer. Dwayne and Perry pulled the pre-labelled bags off the ends of the hoses and were about to throw them down the waste chute when Vip stopped them.

"Wait!" he said. "I want to see inside them."

"No!" cried Perry. "They'll be full of dust and dirt and in Dwayne's case … fireworks."

"I just want to see," said Vip, opening his own bag.

"Don't breathe, Conker," muttered Perry. "Are you feeling sneezy?"

The puppet shook his head.

"Again – me neither. Strange..."

Vip peered inside his bag. He didn't know what he was looking for, but apart from a couple of small lumps of dried-up gel and a few specks of white dust, there wasn't anything in there at all. Slightly disappointed, he opened Perry's. There was a bit more silvery dust but not much else. Dwayne's was the fullest. It smelled of smoke and was packed with a dusty glitter. Vip thought it must have come from the fireworks. He sealed the bags and put them in the hole in the wall. He then went outside to see where the hole led. He found a drawer attached to the bottom of their trailer with the bags resting inside.

"What are you up to?" asked Perry.

"N-nothing," said Vip. "I'm . . . erm . . . just going to go for a walk before bedtime."

"You're not allowed to do that. You'll get in trouble."

"He's creeping round the school," sang Dwayne, *"I think he's lost his mind, the boy's a crazy fool, who knows what he will find."*

"Quiet, Dwayne," hissed Perry. "Vip, get back in this trailer right now."

But Vip had already gone. He ran over to the fountain and hid in the shadow of the huge statue opposite the indigo trailer. A couple of minutes later Melody came out of the door. She looked all around before running over and crouching down beside him.

"Oh my goodness, this is so exciting," she panted. "We're breaking the rules! We're being naughty! I'm never naughty! My mum would be so angry! I should be practising! I don't care! I'm so excited—"

"Melody, shush," whispered Vip. "We're here for a reason."

"Of course," she said. "Sorry. Focus, Melody – if I'm going to be a detective, then I'm going to be a good one."

"Let's just stay in the shadows and wait to see if anyone comes round to collect the bags tonight. Then if they do, we can—"

Vip stopped abruptly at the sound of footsteps on gravel. Voices drifted across the courtyard.

"Oh no, I forgot to put my moon cream on."

"The moon is so beautiful tonight. . ."

Vip sighed and stood up. "Perry! Dwayne! What are you doing here?"

"Following you," said Perry. "What are *you* doing? And Melody! I thought you would know better. You'll get into trouble. Now, come back to the trailers."

"We're seeing what Fenella Stardust does with our hair bags," explained Melody. "Vip thinks she's up to something."

"That's crazy!" cried Perry. "How could she be up to something with some old bags of dust? Come back now. If anyone finds us wandering around at this time then . . . oh no! Someone's coming!"

They all pressed themselves against the wall of the fountain as Fenella Stardust came out of the academy and approached the first trailer. She opened the drawer at the bottom and stuffed several bags into her pocket before moving on to the next one.

"I admit that it's strange that she collects them

herself," whispered Melody. "If she hates dust so much, you would think she would get someone else to do the dirty work."

They watched as she collected all the hair bags from the trailers.

"She's heading back to the main school building," said Vip.

"We have to follow her," added Melody.

"We don't *have* to do anything," cried Perry. "I want you to know that the only reason I'm here is because Conker and Dwayne wanted to come. If it were up to me, I would go straight back to bed. It's cold, it's dark, we're breaking school rules and worst of all, it's a full moon and I haven't got any cream on. I could get moon-burn."

"That's not going to happen, Perry," said Melody. "Besides, we'll be inside."

They waited until Fenella Stardust was safely out of sight before scuttling across the courtyard and into the school. They just saw the tail of her hat disappearing down a spiral staircase, and slowly made their way over. The top of the stairs had a chain across with a staff only sign dangling from the middle.

"That leads to the basement," said Perry, "and it's out of bounds to students. So, now you know where she takes the bags. Let's get out of here."

Vip looked at Melody. "Do you want to go back?" he asked.

"No. Do you?"

"I don't think so. We might as well keep going now we're here. What about you, Dwayne?"

"It's a scary expedition, but my heart's in good condition, and it's really rather thrilling, to be here instead of chilling, so—"

"Shh! Try and keep the noise down, Dwayne," whispered Vip. "Perry, are you coming?"

"He doesn't want to," croaked Conker.

"No, I don't. But someone's got to keep an eye on you lot."

"OK, keep on your toes and press against the wall," said Vip. "Let's go."

They ducked under the chain and down the curling staircase. A warm breeze drifted up from below.

124

"It feels hot down here," breathed Melody.

Vip poked his head around a corner as they got to the bottom. In front of him was a long corridor with several doors leading off it. Fenella Stardust was at the very end with her back to them. He couldn't see what she was doing, and dived back when she began to turn around and walk back towards them.

"It's a dead end," he whispered. "She's coming back again. Quick, up the stairs."

But before they could move, the footsteps stopped and there was the sound of a door opening and closing. Vip peeked around again. The corridor was empty. "She's gone through one of those doors."

Melody stepped out into the corridor. "Let's just see what's at the end," she said, "then we'll go back, OK?"

Perry shook his head but Melody had already gone, closely followed by the other two. A large metal square with a handle was fixed into the wall at the end of the corridor with a red sign above it. As they approached it got hotter and hotter.

"Incinerator," said Melody, reading the sign. "She's burning the bags."

"Of course she is," hissed Perry, catching them up. "What else would she be doing with them? Now, can we please go?"

They turned and tiptoed back along the corridor.

"But it still doesn't make sense," said Vip. "What's the point in labelling the bags if they're going to be burned?"

"Maybe she just likes to know who has the dirtiest hair," whispered Melody. She stopped suddenly, making Vip bump into her.

"What's wrong?" he asked. But he didn't need an answer.

Mr Chalk, the caretaker, was standing at the bottom of the staircase. His hands were on his hips, and his dusty old face was purple with fury.

Mr Chalk

"What do you think you're doing down here, you little scoundrels?" croaked Mr Chalk.

"We were just . . . erm. . ." began Melody.

"Nosing around where you shouldn't be," finished Mr Chalk. His oiled, grey hair was slicked back across his head. He was wearing a brown overcoat with the familiar sequinned SA embroidered on the top pocket. "The basement is out of bounds to students. Do you want to know why?"

"N-no," stammered Perry.

"Well, I'm going to show you!" bellowed the old man.

He led them back along the corridor. They all

followed, terrified that he was going to take them through one of the doors to Fenella Stardust. But he walked past all of them and stopped in front of the large metal square set into the wall. "You," he said, pointing to Perry, "grab hold of the handle and open the door."

"B-but doesn't that lead to the incinerator?" asked Perry.

Mr Chalk turned and glared at him, his pale eyes glistening menacingly. "It would be a shame if your little dolly fell in there then, wouldn't it?"

Suddenly, they all wished that he *was* going to take them to Fenella Stardust. Perry stuffed Conker down his jumper and took hold of the handle with a shaky hand. He pulled but it was stiff.

"Harder!" barked Mr Chalk.

Perry grabbed hold with both hands and tugged with all his might. The small metal door opened with a blast of hot air and a puff of smoke. They all gasped as their hair blew up around their faces.

"All of you look in," Mr Chalk ordered.

Inside, a metal chute disappeared down into a

smouldering red haze. Vip pulled back, his face pink. Melody and Dwayne peeped in, but Perry wouldn't go near. Mr Chalk advanced on him. Perry wrapped his arms around his body, trying to protect Conker.

"Leave him alone!" shouted Melody.

Mr Chalk turned to her. "He needs to understand the danger! If you fell in there, missy, your skin would slide off your bones in a melted slop and your eyes would pop like grapes in a microwave. Even I don't go anywhere near this beast. Fenella Stardust personally takes care of the incinerator herself. Do you all understand?"

They nodded slowly.

"Then get back into your beds and don't let me see you anywhere near this basement again!"

They didn't need telling twice, and ran back up the staircase and out of the doors into the courtyard.

"That was horrible," panted Vip.

"Terrifying!" muttered Perry.

"Alarming!" sang Dwayne.

"Brilliant!" cried Melody. "I've never felt so scared in my life. I loved it!"

The boys stared at her. "And I thought you were a nice, sensible girl," said Perry. "Still, at least we've found out that the bags are destroyed."

Vip frowned. "Maybe you're right," he said. "But why would a famous entertainer, who hates anything dirty, personally take care of the maintenance of an old school incinerator? It still feels wrong."

"There is nothing wrong," sighed Perry. "It's all in your imagination."

"We've all just had a nasty fright," sang Dwayne, *"I think we've done enough tonight."*

"We've done more than enough," said Perry. He disappeared into the magenta trailer closely followed by Dwayne. Vip turned to Melody.

"Thanks," he mumbled, "for helping me do this."

"Thank *you*," she said, "for helping *me* do this." She smiled and tiptoed across to the indigo trailer. "I hope you feel a bit better now. Night, Vip."

"Night."

He crept into his trailer. Olive was asleep on his

duvet. Perry and Conker were climbing into bed and Dwayne was polishing his nose. Vip pulled on his pyjamas and lay next to Olive stroking her beautiful, thick coat. It made him feel calm and seemed to settle his thoughts. Maybe Perry and Melody were right and Fenella Stardust wasn't up to anything suspicious. Everyone thought she was wonderful – everyone except for Olive. And Olive was a very clever cat.

12

The Voice Box

Vip was kept so busy the next day and into the next week, that he almost forgot about his suspicions. The time passed faster than he thought it would. The lessons certainly weren't boring, although he found the dance classes with Mr Poser-Prince unbearable. He had to wear ballet pumps, which was bad enough, and he had done so many pliés – bending down with his knees apart and his head held high – that he now walked like he had been riding a horse his whole life. Olive seemed to like the dance classes though. She was growing in confidence and would parade around the studio weaving in and out of everyone's legs. Mr Poser-

Prince said she had a natural grace and poise that Vip would never have. Music lessons were a bit of a struggle too. Vip had to play the triangle because he was rubbish at everything else, but he did get to hear Melody play which was always brilliant. Miss Stradivarius said that Melody was the best student she had ever taught.

In media studies they had to learn "how to throw shapes for the camera", which Olive was particularly good at, and "how to perform for the paparazzi". It was very embarrassing for Vip and he missed doing English and maths. But it wasn't all bad. He actually quite liked his classmates and could even talk to some of them now. Most were so thrilled to be at Stardust Academy that it was hard not to get caught up in their excitement. However, the live TV show was looming closer. All the lessons were geared towards it. Fenella Stardust kept appearing in their classes and watching them. One evening she arrived at Vip's trailer with a cat-shaped hair-vacuumer, but Olive wouldn't go near it and dashed outside into the school grounds. Fenella Stardust had stormed out of their trailer muttering something about, "it has to be done before the show".

The following morning was their first lesson with Mr Ludwig Van Driver. Dwayne was extremely excited and sang loudly all the way through breakfast. The old teacher came waddling into The Holly wearing a tailed jacket with a neat bow tie. His ruffled shirt frilled out around his pot belly, hiding the top of his smart black trousers. He was carrying a conductor's baton and pointed at every member of Vip's class.

"Good morning, first years," he said in a rich, creamy voice. "It is time for your vocal-vibration lessons. These are held in the Voice Box. Please finish off your breakfast and come with me."

Everybody trooped out of The Holly behind Mr Van Driver. Dwayne and Cherry Dropp were practising their singing scales as the class walked up some steps and through a tunnel lined with fluorescent lights. Mr Van Driver stopped at the far end and pointed his baton proudly at the wall in front of them. An enormous 3D face loomed out.

The mouth of the face was wide open as if it were singing a long, loud note. Mr Van Driver stepped inside the huge lips.

"Look at those chops," whispered Perry. "They're even bigger than Miss Maykova's."

Mr Van Driver beckoned them in. He was standing on a thick, spongy tongue. "Be careful of the teeth," he said. "The canines are quite sharp."

Vip looked around him as he stepped over the row of bottom teeth and into the cave mouth. The roof was ridged in glistening pink ripples. The students all gathered on the thick tongue. Mr Van Driver reached up and pulled on a long dangly thing hanging from above. "The uvula," he explained, giving it a good tug. Immediately, the mouth began to close, trapping them inside. Vip wanted to run and jump out before it shut completely, but nobody moved.

"Now I know how a Cheerio feels," gulped Perry, as the massive lips smacked together, leaving them in a red darkness.

"The Voice Box is soundproof," said Mr Van

Driver, sitting down on the edge of a round hole towards the back of the mouth. "Come along, we need to slide down the throat."

He jumped into the hole and out of sight.

"I'm not going down there," said Perry. "We don't know where it goes."

Melody looked in the hole and smiled. "It's a slide. It obviously leads to the Voice Box." And she dived down head first.

"That one needs to be more careful," said Perry. "My mum says—"

"*Geronimooooooo,*" boomed Dwayne, jumping down the hole after Melody.

"She doesn't say that," Perry continued. "She says—"

But Vip didn't wait to find out what Perry's mum said. He held on to Olive and jumped down the hole too. The slide wasn't as long as he was hoping, and very quickly he slid out into a completely square room. It was windowless and the flesh-coloured walls were padded. It was dominated by a grand piano in the centre. Mr Van Driver was seated at the piano with Melody and Dwayne standing beside him. "Ah, the boy with the cat," said Mr Van Driver as Vip got to his feet. "I remember you from the auditions – Bip, isn't it?"

"It's Vip."

"The cat certainly has potential, but..." He trailed off and looked Vip up and down. "Let's just hope you can find your voice today, young man. By the way, Ms Stardust has specifically asked if Olive can have some private caterwauling classes. Come and see me at the end."

Eventually, everyone came sliding into the room. Perry was last.

"Welcome to the Voice Box," announced Mr Van Driver. "We will start with some warm-up exercises. Join in with me when you're ready... **Bbbbbbbbrrrrrrrrrrrrrrrr!**"

Vip took a step back as Mr Van Driver showered them all with spittle. His lips were pursed together but vibrating wildly as he forced short sharp blasts of air through them. He sounded like an old fashioned telephone. Olive jumped off Vip's shoulder in surprise and scurried under the piano. Slowly everybody started to join in. Vip felt very embarrassed but actually quite enjoyed it once he got going. He looked round at everyone else. He could see Perry's mask vibrating but the "bbbbbbbbbbbbrrrrrrrrrr" appeared to be coming from Conker. Dwayne Pipes was in his element. His lips were vibrating so hard that Vip thought he was going to take off. Gunter Gruber kept adding a little "yodel-ey-he-hoo" in the middle of his bbbrrrrrs, and Pineapple Bunting pirouetted with every one of hers. Mr Van Driver then began singing scales.

"La la la la la la la laaaaaaaaa!" he sang, wobbling his chubby cheeks with his thumb and forefinger as he did so. "Let me hear you. And shake out those cheeks."

"La la la la la la la laaaaaaaaaaaaaa!" sang the class.

"Louder!" shouted Mr Van Driver.

"La la la la la la la laaaaaaaaaaaaa!"

As everyone la-la-la-ed, Mr Van Driver went

around listening to them all individually before holding his baton up for silence. "Not bad, but not good either," he said, opening a door which led to a large storeroom. He went inside and came out a few minutes later carrying several boxes which he put on top of the piano. "Melody and Pineapple, your voices are too high. They need to be lower, more of a rasp to them." He reached into a box and handed them a bowl full of raspberries. "You will stuff your cheeks with these and try again."

The girls looked at each other in surprise before putting a couple of raspberries in their mouths. "More," said Mr Van Driver. "The cheeks need to be packed."

As they stuffed more raspberries in their mouths, Mr Van Driver pointed to Ben Dee, Howl Lafter, Gunter Gruber and Merlin McGandalf. "You boys need to be huskier," he said, handing them a bag of nuts. "Shell these, then put the nuts in the bowl and the husks in your cheeks and try again."

He turned to Dwayne and Cherry. "You are almost perfect, my dears," he said, smiling.

"VOCAL-AMAZEBALLS!" whooped Cherry, hugging Dwayne.

Mr Van Driver handed them a golden jar. "Just a spoonful of honey for you, but be careful it doesn't trickle out whilst you're singing."

Finally, he pointed his baton at Vip and Perry. "You two are a little hoarse," he said. "You need the pony treatment." He handed them a box full of hay.

"But I get hay fever," complained Perry.

"A little sneezing is good for the air passages," said Mr Van Driver. "Come along, stuff it in."

Vip reluctantly began putting pieces of hay in his mouth. It smelled of horse and felt rough against his cheeks. Perry placed some in Conker's mouth, then lifted up his mask and stuffed some in.

"Good!" cried Mr Van Driver, as he looked around at all the bulging cheeks. "Now, after me – *la la la la la la la laaaaaaaaaaaaa!*"

All kinds of snorts and grunts followed but none of them sounded remotely like a "la".

Mr Van Driver looked annoyed. "Not good enough," he snapped. "You need to—"

He stopped at the sound of somebody coming down the slide into the Voice Box. They all turned to see Fenella Stardust spill gracefully into the room. She was closely followed by a very glamorous old lady.

"I'm so sorry to interrupt your class, Mr Van Driver," said Fenella Stardust. "But I have someone very special to introduce to our first years."

"Not at all, Fenella," gushed Mr Van Driver. "And Mrs Cheese! How wonderful to see you again. You look more beautiful every time I see you."

Mr Van Driver and the old lady made noisy "mwah" noises as they pretended to kiss each other on both cheeks.

"My starlets," cried Fenella Stardust, "I would like you to meet my mother, *the* Veronica Cheese!"

Vip stared at the small woman in front of him. She was wrapped up in a black fur cape. Her silver hair was streaked green and piled high on top of her head in elaborate twists and plaits. The mottled skin on her neck and chest was creased together like crêpe paper, contrasting with her taut, stretched face. Her painted eyebrows were pulled so high, she appeared permanently surprised, and when she blinked, her eyelids didn't quite close completely. She surveyed them all with her suspicious, tight eyes.

"Where's the cat?" she wheezed.

13

Veronica Cheese and Dr Doolots

Vip looked frantically around for Olive. She was still under the piano. He was hoping she might see Fenella Stardust and jump through an open window, but the Voice Box didn't have any windows. Veronica Cheese spotted Olive immediately and tottered towards her in a pair of black patent heels.

"Pick it up and let me get a close look at its coat," she commanded.

"Me?" said Fenella Stardust. "But she scratches."

Veronica Cheese glanced at her daughter in disgust. "You're afraid of it," she spat.

"I'm not afraid, Mummy. It's just—"

"Then pick it up!"

But before she could move, Olive had jumped into Vip's arms.

"This is Olive's owner," said Fenella Stardust, looking vaguely at him. "I think he's called Chip."

"It's Vip."

Veronica Cheese didn't acknowledge him at all. She was completely focused on Olive. As she approached them, Vip was engulfed in a cloud of heavy perfume. He wished he was wearing Perry's mask. The old lady reached out a wrinkled hand and began stroking Olive with long, green nails. Vip couldn't move – he could hardly breathe. Olive tensed but remained in his arms as Veronica Cheese parted the fur and ran her hand along Olive's tail. She then looked at her daughter and gave a tiny nod. Fenella Stardust seemed to sigh in relief. "Well, we must be going," she said. "Mummy would like to meet all the classes. She's staying with us until the live TV show as a special hair adviser and then she's flying back to New York."

"How do we get out of here?" asked Veronica Cheese, looking around the room.

"I'm afraid it's back up the slide, Mummy," said Fenella Stardust. "The Voice Box is completely soundproof – no doors or windows allowed."

The old woman sighed and took off her high shoes. "Carry these," she ordered, "and help me get up. I'm not as young as I used to be, although I'm told I could pass for your sister. But I think I look more like your daughter. Have you been using that pork-and-sage face cream I told you to get?"

Fenella Stardust glanced sideways at the listening children.

"I had to stop using it," she whispered. "I smelled like stuffing."

"I don't care if you smelled like a whole roast dinner," snapped Veronica Cheese. "I can see a wrinkle near your lips."

Fenella Stardust gasped and covered her mouth.

"You look terrible!" cried her mother. "Look at me. I'm eighty-seven. Can you see any wrinkles on my face?"

"Um … you look amazing, Mummy," she said,

pushing her mother up the slide. "Doesn't she, everyone?"

There were a few murmurs and a loud "yes" from Mr Van Driver as Veronica Cheese disappeared inside the hole in the wall, closely followed by her daughter. Everyone watched them go.

"Did you see that?" whispered Melody. "Fenella Stardust is terrified of her mother. Who'd have thought?"

"I don't blame her," said Perry. "But they both seem to love Olive."

Vip nodded grimly. "I've realized that it's her coat they love. I think they want her fur!"

Melody and Perry looked at him in horror, but before they could say anything Mr Van Driver began tapping his baton on the piano.

"Right!" he cried. "Back to work, please, Class. Raspberries, husks, honey and hay in mouths, and . . . *la la la la la la laaaaaaaaaaaaaaaaaaaaaaaaaaaaa!*"

Vip found it hard to concentrate on the rest of the lesson. In fact, he found it hard to concentrate on any of his lessons after that. He kept Olive close to him and never let her out of his sight, just in case he was right about Fenella Stardust and her mother. Melody and Perry weren't so sure. Melody had even plucked up the courage at dinner one night to ask Fenella Stardust if her hats were real fur. But she had just smiled and said that she was an animal lover. Vip thought she might be a dead animal lover.

Sometimes Fenella Stardust would sit in on Vip's animal-training lessons. He had them once a week with a teacher called Dr Doolots. No one else in his year had a pet, so Vip was put in a special class with a boy from the second year who had a gerbil circus, twins from the third year with their identical singing wombats and a girl from the fourth year who had trained worms to weave themselves into friendship bracelets.

Fenella Stardust sat at the back of the classroom, her usual aroma of coffee and carrots drifting to the front, making the wombats sneeze. "Pretend I'm not here, Dr Doolots," she said. "I'm just observing today. Have all the animals been cleaned and de-flead? You know how sensitive I am."

"I de-flead the worms myself, madam," said Dr Doolots, "and the gerbils are squeaky clean." He held up a gerbil, which squealed gently as if to prove his point. He was a tall man with a large forehead and lots of hair which made him look even taller. All the animals adored him and seemed to understand every word he said. Olive would purr loudly whenever he gave her his full attention. Vip felt a tiny bit jealous at first.

"Look into your animal's eyes," he told the class.

Vip glanced down at Olive's yellow eyes. He couldn't help noticing that the girl in the fourth year was turning her worms around, not sure which end to look at.

"Make them feel comfortable and relaxed," said Dr Doolots, tickling the wombats' tummies. Vip was sure he heard one of the wombats giggle. He put Olive on his lap and looked around. The circus gerbils were curled up, one on top of the other to form a small gerbil pyramid, and worm-girl was singing softly to a pile of soil.

"Worms are like cats," Dr Doolots went on. "They want to be in control. Treat them like they're the boss and they'll do anything for you. Wombats however, need a lot more attention and guidance. They're very sensitive and need lots of positive encouragement. Never insult your wombats."

"Yes, Dr Doolots," said the twins in unison.

"And then we have the gerbils," said Dr Doolots. "Known for their extreme loyalty and high intelligence, they are energetic, watchful, fearless and obedient; but make sure you keep them stimulated – a bored gerbil is a dangerous gerbil."

Vip looked over at the sleeping balls of fluff. Their owner was nodding vigorously in agreement.

"Understanding your animal is the key to training them," continued Dr Doolots. "How did you train your cat, Vip?"

Vip blushed as everyone turned to stare at him.

"I-I've never trained Olive to do anything," he said. "She just sort of does things."

"Exactly!" cried Dr Doolots. "You have a natural way with animals, Vip. I like that."

Vip smiled. Dr Doolots was the first teacher who had made him feel really welcome.

"We've seen how Olive can pick locks that require a key," continued Dr Doolots. "Let's see if she can work out a combination lock."

He handed Vip a padlock which had a set of three rotating numbers instead of a key. In order to open the lock, the numbers had to be set in a correct sequence. Vip showed Olive how to turn the numbers. He was aware that Fenella Stardust was watching closely. Olive sniffed it and then began to paw the numbers, making a strange high-pitched noise as she did so. At first Vip thought she was hissing but Dr Doolots noticed it too and started smiling.

"I do believe your cat is whistling while she works," he chuckled. "Good work, Vip."

Vip didn't know why Olive had started to

whistle. Maybe it was because they shared a trailer with Dwayne or maybe it was Mr Van Driver's caterwauling classes. Either way, Fenella Stardust was very impressed.

"Bravo, Olive," she cried from the back of the class. "A whistling cat!"

Vip's heart sank. This might encourage her to pick them for the TV show. "Shh, Olive," he whispered.

But Olive seemed to like whistling and there was nothing he could do to stop her. However, much to his relief, she couldn't open the lock. She gave up and began to lick Vip's ears instead.

"Not bad for a first attempt," said Dr Doolots. "Keep practising."

Vip couldn't hear him properly. It was hard with a small pink tongue in his ear. But Olive did keep practising. She practised that night and the following day and every day, right up to the half-term holidays. She loved the padlock and would knock it across the floor like a ping-pong ball and pounce on it. When Vip went home for the holiday break, she played with it every day and by the time they went back to school she could open it. Vip couldn't help feeling proud of her. But he decided to keep her combination-lock abilities to himself, at least until after the TV show.

14

Devouring Olives

The first couple of weeks after half term passed without incident. Dance lessons were still embarrassing and painful and painfully embarrassing, but Vip had to admit that he actually enjoyed some of the classes. Even the teachers were beginning to remember his name. Animal training with Dr Doolots was great fun and Olive loved it. Howl always had the whole class in fits of giggles during their stand-up comedy classes, and Merlin actually disappeared right in front of their eyes in the middle of a "Stealing the Show" lesson. There was a rumour flying round that he might actually be a real wizard. Merlin himself refused to comment.

Vip started to realize that with all these talented children in his class alone, there was no chance that he and Olive would get chosen for the TV show. Fenella Stardust seemed to be leaving them alone and he began to relax. Maybe it was just his imagination and she wasn't after Olive's coat at all.

He sat on his pink bed and looked around at his room-mates. Dwayne was lying down with his eyes closed and Perry had just finished dazzling his nails.

"Dwayne's lost his voice," said Perry, pointing at him with a gleaming finger. "He says he feels drained. I'm tired too and Conker is exhausted. I was thinking about taking my mask off the other day but I'm worried there might be a bug going round. Melody looked really pale at dinner tonight."

"Maybe it was the pigeon pie," said Vip, "although she didn't look good during our 'Perfect Selfie' class this afternoon."

He looked out of his window and saw Melody near the huge statue of Fenella Stardust. She was throwing stones into the fountain. He wanted to go and see if she was all right, but he knew they weren't supposed to go out at this time. He glanced down at Olive, who was sleeping peacefully on his duvet, and very carefully pulled the cover around her so she was hidden from view.

"I'm just going to see if Olive is outside," he murmured.

"But she was right here, asleep on your bed," said Perry, "and you're not allowed..."

Vip didn't stop to listen and closed the trailer door behind him before dashing across the courtyard towards Melody.

"Hi," he whispered.

She turned to face him. Her cheeks were pale and damp.

"What's wrong?"

"I can't do it," she sniffed.

"Do what?"

"Play the violin."

"Of course you can. You're brilliant!"

"I keep going wrong," sobbed Melody. "I feel exhausted, and the more I practise, the more mistakes I keep making. Miss Stradivarius says I'll never become a world-class violin player at this rate. She thinks I haven't been practising but I have, all the time."

"I know you have," said Vip. "We can hear you from our trailer . . . it's great."

"It's not great," snapped Melody. "It's rubbish!"

Vip didn't know what to say. He stood beside her and began throwing stones into the fountain too. "Remember," he said, eventually, "you Milliken girls can do anything. . ."

Melody turned and smiled. "Sorry for snapping."

"Perry says there's a bug going round," said Vip. "Lots of people are feeling tired."

"Maybe that's it. Come on, we'd better get back to our trailers. It's hair-bag collection tonight and we don't want to get caught outside again."

They turned to go but stopped as the door to the academy swung open and the voice of Fenella Stardust drifted into the night air. "I've got a good crop this year," she said.

Vip and Melody shrank against the fountain as she approached the first trailer and stuffed the hair bags in her pocket. Her mother was with her.

"Has anyone noticed that they're becoming less talented?" asked Veronica Cheese.

"I make sure that I only take a little bit, so it's not obvious. However, some of the first years are becoming very tired. That girl I was telling you about, the violin player? She has started making mistakes."

Melody let out a little gasp.

"You've taken too much, you silly girl," said Veronica Cheese. "She's one of your most talented students and you need her to get better for the TV special. It's coming up in a few of weeks. Don't take any more for the rest of term. And what about the cat?"

"Olive?"

"What sort of a name is that? She should be called Ebony or Jet, something to match that magnificent coat."

"I suppose olives can be black and shiny, too."

"Perhaps . . . and I do love devouring olives."

Vip's jaw tensed. Were they planning on eating his cat?

157

"She's covered in the stuff," continued Fenella Stardust. "But I can't get my hands on her . . . yet."

"Well, try harder!" barked her mother. "They've been here for weeks. Do you want to lose everything? Do you want to fade into obscurity?"

Fenella Stardust didn't reply, but shook her head. Vip and Melody watched from the shadows as they went from trailer to trailer collecting the bags and eventually disappeared back inside.

"She's taking something from you," whispered Vip. "And that's why you're feeling so tired. But what can it be?"

"There's only one way to find out," said Melody. "Let's follow them, and no getting caught this time."

They waited a minute before creeping into the school and down the spiral staircase.

"Wait," whispered Melody as they got to the bottom of the stairs. "I've got this." She produced a small hand mirror. "We can use it for seeing round corners. All the best detectives have them. . ."

She poked the mirror around the corner and they both watched as Fenella Stardust put the bags into the incinerator. "Nobody will ever suspect," she said to her mother. "I've convinced them all that I have a thing about dust."

"Well, you do," cackled Veronica Cheese. "Just not in the way they think."

Fenella Stardust started laughing too as they disappeared through a nearby door.

Vip and Melody looked at each other in amazement.

"You were right," hissed Melody. "She *is* up to something. Come on, let's take a closer look at that incinerator."

"But Mr Chalk—"

"Do you want to find out what's going on?"

"Yes, but—"

"So let's go!"

He watched her tiptoe down the corridor with a mixture of exasperation and admiration. Her mother was right. Those Milliken girls *could* do anything. He crept after her and looked on as she pulled open the metal door and peered inside the incinerator.

"It's hot in there," she said, "but not as hot as it should be for an incinerator. Lower me down the chute, I want to have a closer look."

"What?"

"Grab hold of my ankles," she said, heaving her top half inside the metal doorway. "I want to see where this slide leads."

"No," hissed Vip. "It leads to the incinerator. You'll be burnt to a crisp. You heard what Mr Chalk said."

"Just do it!"

Reluctantly, Vip caught hold of Melody's ankles as she lowered herself down. He was terrified she was going to fall. Beads of perspiration trickled down his forehead, stinging his eyes.

"OW!" yelled Melody.

Vip immediately began pulling her up. "You're burning!"

"No I'm not. You're squeezing my ankles so hard, I can't feel my toes. I need to go down further. I can see something beyond the red glow. . ."

Vip was concentrating so hard on holding tightly

to Melody's legs that he didn't hear the footsteps behind him. A hand clamped around his shoulder. He jumped and cried out as Melody's ankles slid through his grasp and she disappeared down the chute.

15

Carrots, Coffee, Cocoa and Tights

"You've just killed Melody!" cried a voice behind him.

Vip spun round to see Perry ripping off his surgical mask. His mouth was wide open, forming a silent scream. Vip felt numb. "No!" he wailed, sticking his head through the metal door. "Melody! Melody!"

"Yes?" came her voice from down below.

"Melody?"

"I'm OK," she called. "Come on. There's no incinerator, but you have to see what's down here."

Vip turned to face Perry. "She's all right," he breathed. "Thank goodness. But what are you doing here?"

"What am *I* doing here?" spluttered Perry. "Conker and I are looking after you two lunatics, that's what!"

Perry thrust Conker in front of Vip. His painted eyebrows were pushed together in an angry frown. Vip looked past the puppet at Perry. It was the first time he had seen Perry's whole face and he couldn't help staring at his wide mouth and polished nose.

"We had to come back," said Vip. "We found out that Fenella Stardust is taking something from the students. Her mother said that she had taken too much from Melody and that's why she's been making lots of mistakes in music. We have to slide down here." He pointed to the incinerator door.

"No way! It's too dangerous."

"You heard what Melody said. There is no incinerator."

"But it's still hot and I have very sensitive skin."

"When was the last time you used your moon cream, Perry?"

"Weeks ago."

"Candle cream? Torch cream?"

"Same."

"And how's your skin?"

"Fine."

"Exactly! I think you probably only need some sunscreen when it's hot, just like everyone else. You're healthier than you think you are."

Melody's voice drifted out of the incinerator. "Is that Perry?" she asked. "It's so nice to hear that he's finally breaking away from his mother's paranoia. But do you think you could stop chatting and join me?"

Perry peered down the chute and then back at Vip. "What's paranoia?"

"I don't know," answered Vip. "Maybe it's like paragliding or parachuting or—"

"My mum doesn't have a parachute."

"Will you two stop faffing around and just get down here!" shouted Melody in frustration.

"That one is trouble," muttered Perry.

"I know," said Vip, pulling himself through the door and looking down at the orange glow below him. "But I kind of like it."

He pushed himself down the chute. The metal

164

slide was very warm. Vip was worried it might singe his trousers as he slid into the haze. He closed his eyes and was surprised when he landed on a hard floor a minute later. Melody pulled him to his feet. They were surrounded by a red mist that came up to their knees.

"It's dry ice," she explained. "It's harmless. They use it in stage shows. Look, it's lit up by these red and orange lights."

Vip looked up at the ceiling which was covered in glowing spotlights. They were in a small round room with an archway leading out at one end.

"And that is why it's so hot," she continued, pointing to a large heater which was pumping scorching air up the chute. "This is all fake. It's been set up to look like an incinerator to keep people away. I landed in this." She held up a wicker basket full of hair bags.

Vip shook his head in amazement. "Come on, Perry," he called. "I promise, it's fine down here."

He jumped out of the way as Perry came sliding down, holding his nose.

"He's not wearing his mask," whispered Melody.

"He ripped it off in shock when he thought I'd killed you," answered Vip. "I don't think he's even noticed, so don't say anything."

Perry got to his feet and looked around him. "I don't believe it!"

"It gets stranger through here," said Melody, leading them out of the dry ice and through the archway.

They stepped out into a large room. Half of it was taken up by what appeared to be an underground field. Huge sunlamps beamed down on to rows of growing vegetation.

"Carrots!" announced Perry. "My mum grows them in our garden. She says they'll help my eyesight. Look, some have already been harvested."

Several baskets of carrots stood in a row under a wall of shelving on the other side of the room. Vip picked one up and then looked up at the shelves. They were stacked full of packets of cocoa and jars of coffee. Above them were rows of hair bags all neatly labelled with different people's names.

"She *is* doing something with the hair bags!" cried Vip. "I knew it!"

"Look at this," said Melody, pointing to a washing line which ran the length of the room. Several pairs of skin-coloured tights were neatly pegged to the line. There were two doors at either end of the room. One of them was painted gold and had a glass handle which looked like a huge diamond. The lock was star-shaped. Vip put his ear to the golden door and could hear a strange bubbling and gurgling noise coming from the other side. He tentatively turned the diamond handle. It was locked. Perry was just about to examine the other door when the sound of footsteps and voices drifted from underneath.

"There's someone coming," he hissed. "Hide."

Vip and Melody dived down in the carrot field and Perry hid behind one of the baskets as Fenella Stardust and her mother entered the room. Vip held his breath as they walked towards the shelving. Fenella Stardust picked out a couple of carrots from the basket that Perry was hiding behind. She held

167

them up to the light and inspected them before grabbing a packet of cocoa, a jar of coffee and three hair bags. Her mother was unpegging a pair of tights from the washing line.

"Are they American-tan?" she asked.

"Of course," replied Fenella Stardust. "I know what I'm doing, Mummy."

She reached up around her neck and took off the glittering star that Vip had noticed the first time he came to the academy. She put it in the golden door with the diamond handle.

"It's a key," whispered Melody.

Vip watched as the pair disappeared into the room beyond. As soon as the door closed Perry jumped up from his hiding place. "Let's get out of here!"

"Wait," said Melody. "Now's our chance to see what's through that door."

"She's crazy!" yelped Perry. "I don't want to get caught in Fenella Stardust's carrot wonderland."

"Keep your voice down, Perry," whispered Vip. "You're right, though. I think we should go while we can. Now we know how to get here, we can come back another time. We might even be able to *borrow* the star-key and find out exactly what's happening behind that door. The best detectives know when to call it a day, Melody."

"OK," she agreed, "but we have to get that key. I bet we can get back to the main school through the other door."

They tiptoed across the room, opened the door and walked out into a hallway, straight into Mr Chalk.

16

Chalk and Cheese

Mr Chalk was as surprised to see the children as they were to see him. He jumped back in shock.

"You again!" he growled. "What do you think you're doing in there? Those are Fenella Stardust's private apartments. No one is allowed in."

"W-we didn't mean to," said Melody. "We fell into the incinerator by accident and it isn't an incinerator at all, it's a—"

"What are you talking about?" shouted Mr Chalk. "You have crept down here to the lower levels of the school, knowing full well that it's strictly out of bounds. I've let you off once but not again. I'm taking you to my office to wait there till I find Ms Stardust and tell her what you've done."

He ushered them along the hallway and through a door with his name on into a small room. There was a desk against one wall and an old squishy sofa by another. "You sit there till I come back," he commanded. "And no funny business while I'm gone."

He stared at them with his cloudy, old eyes, before shutting the door behind him.

"What if we get expelled?" wailed Perry. "My mum will go mad."

"Not as mad as mine," sniffed Melody.

Vip hadn't thought about getting expelled. His parents would be angry too. The thought of leaving Stardust Academy wasn't as appealing as it once was. He'd actually made friends, and despite everything, he really wanted to stay.

He looked around the room. The walls were covered in photos and framed certificates and old newspaper articles. Melody was already on her feet studying a picture.

"Wow!" she cried. "Look at this."

It was a black-and-white photo of Mr Chalk. His hair was still greased back but it was jet black and there was a lot more of it. He was wearing a tailed dinner jacket and carrying a top hat in one hand and a cane in the other. But the most surprising thing about the photo was the woman linking arms with him – a very young Fenella Stardust, dressed in a long ballgown. Perry looked at a framed certificate next to the photo. "It's an award," he said. "Best newcomers at the national TV awards – Chalk and Cheese!"

"Chalk and Cheese?" repeated Vip. "I've heard of them before. My mum and dad said Fenella Stardust used to be in a double act before hitting the big time on her own."

"Of course," said Melody. "Cheese is her mother's name. She must have changed hers to Stardust."

"And Mr Chalk was her partner," added Perry. "Blimey! I wonder how he ended up being her caretaker?"

They continued looking at all the old photos and

reading the newspaper clippings. Chalk and Cheese had started out very successfully. They were a comic song-and-dance act. They had even had their own show a very long time ago.

"Listen to this," said Vip, reading a news article. "'The Chalk and Cheese Show is to be cancelled after only two series. According to sources close to the duo, Gerry Chalk, the driving force and comic genius behind the show's success, is said to be suffering from severe fatigue. This was clearly evident in the last few episodes of their show. Mr Chalk appeared to forget some of the steps in their dance routines, and his voice had lost that velvety—'"

He stopped as Mr Chalk stepped back into the room. He eyed them all suspiciously. "Nosying around again?"

"We couldn't help but notice some of your awards," said Melody. "We didn't realize that you used to be a performer too. You were obviously very good."

Mr Chalk seemed to soften, and looked around

the room nodding. "I *was* good but that was a lifetime ago. . ."

"You should be a teacher here," she continued.

He gave a wry smile. "I've got nothing to teach. I can't do anything any more."

Melody pointed at one of the old newspaper cuttings. "Comic genius, it says here."

"Any talent I may have had left me a long time ago and I haven't performed for years. Luckily for me, my old partner felt sorry for me and gave me this job at her academy. I owe Fenella Stardust a lot."

"Talent doesn't just disappear," said Melody.

"Yes it does," replied Mr Chalk. "I've seen it happen to lots of students over the years. One minute they're the next big thing. Then gradually they become drained, exhausted, washed up. Strange, really. . ."

Mr Chalk frowned and seemed to jump back into caretaker mode. "I don't even know why I'm telling you this," he snapped. "You're just trying to get round me so that I won't tell Ms Stardust where you've been. She's going to be furious. But luckily for you, she's currently using her self-tanning machine and cannot be disturbed. So, I'm going to take you back to your trailers and inform her in the morning."

They followed him out of the office and up a set of stairs into the corridor where the entrance to the incinerator was. Melody hesitated as Mr Chalk headed towards the spiral staircase.

"Mr Chalk," she said. "You must believe us. There's no incinerator down there."

He stopped and turned around. "I'll have no more of your lies, missy. I've been at this academy since it opened and I would know if there wasn't an incinerator."

"Have you ever seen it?" she asked.

Mr Chalk paused for a moment. "I've seen down the chute and that's enough. Ms Stardust looks after the incinerator personally."

"Shouldn't that be your job?" continued Melody.

Vip looked at Melody in awe. He could never talk to an adult like that. But she was obviously making Mr Chalk think. His furrowed forehead revealed deep worry lines.

"You have a lot to say for such a small girl," he said. "For your information, Ms Stardust looks after the incinerator so that I can take care of more important things like the maintenance of the school and making sure nosy students don't go anywhere they shouldn't!"

"Good try," whispered Vip as they followed Mr Chalk out of the main school building.

He couldn't say any more to her because Mr Chalk waited in the courtyard to make sure that they went back inside their trailers. The boys gently opened the front door and crept inside to find Dwayne standing in the middle of the room with his hands on his hips. Although he only came up to Vip's shoulder, he looked quite menacing.

"It's nearly eleven!
Where have you been?"
     he blasted in his loudest baritone boom.
"You left me alone,
and that's really mean."

"No, Dwayne," said Vip. "It wasn't like that. I only went outside to see if Melody was all right and then one thing led to another. Come and sit down and we'll tell you everything."

Vip and Perry told Dwayne all about the fake incinerator, the strange carrot room and the photos and newspaper articles they saw in Mr Chalk's office. Dwayne wasn't very happy. He adored Fenella Stardust.

> "Ms Stardust likes carrots! That's not suspicious,
> I like them myself, and cocoa's delicious.
> How could you think she was up to no good?
> When all that she's doing is eating nice food."

"You didn't see it," said Perry. "It was weird. I wish I'd never seen it. I wish I'd stayed here with you."

He sighed and climbed into bed.

"Are you OK, Perry?" whispered Vip.

"I'm just worried," he replied. "I don't want to be expelled. My mum really wants me to become famous so that we can get lots of 'ologists' to help with my allergies."

"Do you realize that you haven't had your mask on all night?"

"What?" Perry sat up suddenly in bed and put his hands to his mouth in shock. "Where is it?"

"You ripped it off when you thought Melody had fallen into the incinerator, but you didn't even notice. How are you feeling?"

"Erm . . . OK, I think," said Perry.

"Sneezy?"

"No."

"Breathless?"

"No."

"Itchy?"

"No, I feel fine."

"Great," said Vip, pulling on his pyjamas. "Let's see how you feel in the morning. And try not to worry about tomorrow. I don't think we'll get expelled. We can just say we got lost."

He went into the bathroom, brushed his teeth and watched them glow. He didn't want Perry to know that he was really worried too. What was Fenella Stardust going to say when she found out that they had been in her private apartments? This could be his last night at Stardust Academy.

17

The Celebrity Circus Tent

Fenella Stardust didn't say anything at all to Vip, Perry and Melody the following morning. They watched her closely at breakfast but she didn't even look their way.

"Mr Chalk obviously hasn't told her yet," sniffed Perry, as they finished their food and made their way to the gym. "I bet she'll grab us at lunch."

Nobody had any energy during Mr Robust's PE class. He told them that they were seriously lacking P-M-A, and kept them back for five minutes after class to do twenty star-jumps whilst shouting, "I am a star!"

Afterwards they filed into The Holly for lunch. Fenella Stardust was sitting at a table with her mother, eating kitty-crackers. She looked up as the class arrived but appeared to be in deep conversation and didn't take much notice of anyone.

"I reckon we might have got away with it," whispered Melody, as they sat down at a table. "Maybe Mr Chalk found out that we weren't lying about the incinerator and hasn't said anything."

"Well, he certainly wasn't lying about Fenella Stardust using her fake tan last night," added Perry. "Look at the colour of her."

Vip glanced over. She was bright orange. He quickly looked down as Veronica Cheese caught his eye and hurriedly whispered something in her daughter's ear. Fenella Stardust put down her cracker and came over. "Ah, I've been looking for you," she called.

They all froze.

"Melody," she continued, "Miss Maykova has mentioned that your hair is becoming rather dry."

Vip glanced sideways at Melody. This wasn't what they were expecting.

"Oh ... um ... really?"

"Yes, really," she continued, "so I would like you to stop using the hair-vacuumers for the rest of term."

"Yes, Miss."

"And keep practising the violin. You're in with a good chance of appearing on the TV show. It's in three weeks' time, so I will be deciding exactly who will be performing by the end of this week. Now, hurry up and eat your kitty-crackers. You don't want to be late for afternoon lessons."

"Yes, Miss."

They all crammed in their crackers and dashed out of The Holly as quickly as they could. As soon as they were out of earshot, Vip turned to the other two.

"That proves it!" he cried. "Veronica Cheese told Fenella Stardust not to take anything from you for the rest of term and now you're not allowed to use the hair vacuumers. There's more than just dust in those bags."

"This is crazy," said Melody. "We have to get that star-key and find out exactly what's going on."

Perry looked sick.

"It's impossible," he wailed. "And Conker doesn't want to go back again."

"Come on, Conker," said Melody, grabbing the puppet. "We have to finish what we've started."

Perry snatched him back. "You're lucky that Conker and I are always around to keep you out of trouble."

"It doesn't work though," laughed Melody.

"She's a bad influence," grumbled the puppet.

"I agree," said Perry. He wasn't wearing his mask again, and it turned out that they still couldn't see his lips move when Conker talked. It was slightly unnerving.

They ran to their next class, "Gushing with Gusto", and spent the rest of the afternoon learning the correct terminology to use when flattering a colleague and how to make an emotional speech if they were ever in an award-ceremony situation. Cherry Dropp became hysterical after delivering a pretend acceptance speech and had to be taken to the medical room. Vip couldn't give the lesson his full attention. He was too busy thinking how to get hold of the star-key.

His chance came along a few days later. A huge marquee had been erected in the academy gardens. It was called the Celebrity Circus Tent and was where *Fenella Stardust's Showbiz Extravaganza* was to be filmed. Every class could use the tent for one afternoon a week to practise their own individual acts. Fenella Stardust was going to watch their performances and pick who she wanted to appear on the show. It was the turn of Vip's class and he was dreading it. He now had a range of cages, boxes and safes, which Olive was quite competent at opening. Fenella Stardust watched closely as Olive took a sparkly necklace out of one safe and deposited it in another.

"I just love the whistling," she said. "It's unique. I don't think I've ever heard a cat whistle before."

She bent over and peered closely at Olive. The star-shaped key was hanging around her neck on a chain and dropped out of her silk shirt. It was centimetres from Vip's hand. Olive sniffed it. She seemed to like shiny things. Fenella Stardust turned to Vip. "You, erm . . . Drip?"

"Vip."

"Yes, well, you really need to clear up Olive's catty dandruff." She stood up straight and tucked the key back into her top. "She was obviously scared of the cat-shaped vacuumer, so I'm having a special brush made for her. It is attached to a hose and will suck up any dandruff as you brush her. It's not ready yet but I'll let you know as soon as it is. I might not be able to use her in the TV show unless this problem is sorted."

"Better not sort it then," whispered Vip, as Fenella Stardust moved on to watch Merlin McGandalf saw himself in half. Perry came over. He was blowing a huge bubble. "How did that go?" he asked.

"The star-key fell out of her shirt," said Vip. "I could almost touch it . . . why are you blowing bubbles?"

"It's my latest act. My mum is going to have a fit when she sees I'm not wearing a surgical mask. I tried to tell her that I'm not allergic to anything but she won't listen. She never listens. So to keep her happy, I'm going to perform inside a giant bubble. No germs can get in a bubble."

"How are you going to get inside?"

He pointed to a large tub of soapy water. "Conker is going to blow a huge bubble from the inside rather than the outside."

"Conker? That's impossible!"

"So is a whistling, lock-picking cat, but you seem to have one."

"True," agreed Vip. "Hey, that's given me an idea . . . No, too dangerous."

"What?"

"No, I couldn't risk Olive."

"Tell me."

"I was just wondering if Olive could steal the key. . ."

"Could you train her to do that?"

"I've never *trained* her to do anything. I was just going to ask her."

"What does Melody think?"

"I'll tell her at dinner."

*

186

Melody thought it was a great idea, so Vip asked Olive, very politely, if she could steal the key from around Fenella Stardust's neck. However, the next morning she did a wee inside their trailer. Vip thought it might be her way of complaining, so he didn't ask her again and continued to rack his brains on how to get the key himself.

At the end of the week Fenella Stardust called for a special assembly to announce who would be performing with her on *Fenella Stardust's Showbiz Extravaganza*. The whole school gathered in The Holly. It was only two weeks till Christmas and the huge holly bushes were garlanded with gold, silver and pink tinsel to match the school colours. A massive Christmas tree rose up in the centre. A large angel with the face of Fenella Stardust sat on the top.

"How are you feeling since you stopped vacuuming your hair?" Vip asked Melody.

"Brilliant," she said. "I'm not making any mistakes at all and I don't feel tired either."

Fenella Stardust tapped a glass to get everyone's attention and then switched on a microphone, inspecting it closely. "Has the microphone been bleached?" she asked.

"Twice today," called Mr Chalk from the back of the room.

"Wonderful," she said. "OK, my starlets, it's time for the announcement you've all been waiting for."

Everybody fell silent. Vip could see that lots of students had their fingers crossed, hoping to be picked. He did the same but for the opposite reason.

"It has been a tough decision," continued Fenella Stardust. "You've all been working very hard this term. The more you practise the more talented you become, which is a great thing for me ... and you, of course. But for this particular TV show, I have decided to showcase some of our first years."

"SUPERB-ERAMI!" screamed Cherry, jumping on the table. She produced a large pair of gold pom-poms and waved them in the air, kicking her legs high above her shoulders. "Go first years! Go first years! Go first years!"

There was a collective moan from all the other year groups, and Vip.

"Don't be too disappointed, my starlets," said Fenella Stardust. "There will be other TV shows where you will get a chance to perform with me. The good news is you and your families will be part of the audience. Every parent and child has a ticket booked and paid for by me."

A polite round of applause filtered around the room. Fenella Stardust waited for Cherry to climb down from the table before she continued to speak.

"Now, the acts that I have chosen to perform are. . ."

There it was again, thought Vip. That horrible word – *perform*.

"Melody Milliken, Perry Winkle, and the amazing Olive . . . accompanied by her handler."

Vip watched as Cherry's gold pom-pom dropped from her hand and rolled across the floor like a ball of tumbleweed. He knew they were both feeling the same way – totally devastated, for very different reasons.

18

Stardust

The two weeks leading up to the TV show were taken up with rehearsals in the Celebrity Circus Tent. Fenella Stardust had devised a performance for Olive and herself. Vip had to be part of it as Olive refused to do anything without him. Fenella Stardust was going to dress up as Queen Elizabeth the First and perform a song-and-dance routine celebrating how beautiful and glorious and royal she was. Then she would pretend to fall asleep on her throne. Vip had to creep in dressed as the court jester with Olive on his shoulder. Olive had to steal her crown and deliver it to Vip who was to lock it up in a wooden chest. Then Fenella Stardust/Elizabeth I would wake up and catch them. She would ask a member of the audience if they could open the chest. After it had been shown to be impossible, Olive herself would open it and deliver the crown back to Fenella Stardust/Elizabeth I, who would then pretend to chop off Vip's head and finally adopt Olive.

Vip hated it. Fenella Stardust wanted him to sing "Losing My Mind" while he was getting his head chopped off. But he kept forgetting the words and his voice cracked with every attempt.

"I'm beginning to think I've made the wrong choice," she grumbled at the final dress rehearsal. "I knew I was taking a chance, but now even the cat's stopped whistling. I should have picked Gunter Gruber. He would have made a wonderful yodelling Shakespeare. I need to think. Let's take a five minute break."

Vip wandered over to where Melody and Perry were watching from the side. He wished with all his heart that Fenella Stardust *had* picked Gunter. The live TV show was tomorrow and he was having sleepless nights.

"This is a nightmare," he said. "How am I ever going to get out of this?"

"We could still stop the show," said Melody. "If we could only prove that Fenella Stardust is up to something."

"But that's not fair on you two," replied Vip.

"I told you, I don't care about being famous. I just want to be a brilliant violinist."

"And I don't need to be famous now that I'm completely allergy free," said Perry. "No 'ologists' required."

Vip wanted to hug them both. "Thanks," he sighed. "But I think it's too late. Our parents have their tickets booked and are really excited, the film and lighting crews are setting up already . . . and we are never going to get that star-key."

Vip watched nervously as Perry and Melody practised their routines for the show. Melody played a piece called *Meditation* accompanied by Mr Van Driver on the piano. It gave Vip goose bumps. Perry had an enormous tub filled with soapy water. He had given up attempting to blow bubbles from

Conker. Instead he had an extra-large hoop which he dipped in the bath and then whooshed it up around his body, enclosing himself and Conker inside. Conker's voice was slightly muffled but after a few attempts Vip could hear him clearly. It was very impressive. When they finally finished rehearsing, Fenella Stardust called them all over.

"Be careful with that water, Perry," she said. "Make sure you don't splash me. It would ruin my outfit. I'm only allowing it because it's essential for your act. Melody, you need to smile more while you're playing. This is a Christmas show, not a funeral. And you..." she turned to Vip. "We shall have to keep your performance to a minimum. No singing, just be there for Olive and try not to ruin everything."

As they ran back to their trailers, Vip hoped that that would be the last he saw of Fenella Stardust for the day. But that evening, she knocked on their door. "I've brought Olive a present," she said. Olive immediately hid under the bed as she produced a cat brush with a hose and a bag attached to it. "She must be vacuumed tonight. This is a much quieter device so it shouldn't scare her."

To Vip's surprise, Olive came out from under the bed and padded towards Fenella Stardust, who held out her hand in delight. Olive climbed up her arm on to her shoulder and sniffed her fur hat. Fenella Stardust fumbled for the switch on her modified cat brush but the moment Olive saw it, she took off through the open door.

"Blast that cat!" she shouted, turning round to face Vip. "*You* must vacuum her. She's never going to trust me."

She threw the brush at Vip and stormed out of the trailer. Almost immediately, Olive came strolling back in. She rubbed herself against Vip's legs. As he bent down to pick her up, she dropped something into his hand. He looked down to see the sparkling star-key. So that was why she had jumped up on to Fenella Stardust. Clever old Olive.

"Is she all right?" asked Perry.

"Yes, fine," said Vip, closing his fist quickly to hide the star-key. He didn't want Perry or Melody getting into any more trouble because of him. He was going to find out what was behind that door himself.

Vip waited until Perry and Dwayne were asleep, then tiptoed out of the trailer and through the academy down to the fake incinerator. He was hoping that Olive would stay in the trailer but she seemed to understand that he was on an important mission and remained close to his heels. He picked her up and slid down into the room with the underground carrot field and crept past the shelves of cocoa, coffee, tights and hair bags. He put his ear against the golden door with the diamond handle before gently sliding the star-key into place and clicking it open. Olive jumped up on to his shoulder as he cautiously walked into a long room lined with mirrors. In the middle was a glass shower cubicle and at the far end an enormous brick fireplace housed a large cauldron which bubbled and hissed over an open flame. Vip studied the shower cubicle.

"I thought she didn't like washing with water," he murmured to Olive.

He crept past a table with a mixing bowl and several metal canisters on top. Folded neatly beside them were three pairs of paper pants and a vest. He peered into the cauldron. A murky orange liquid popped and sizzled inside. A strong carroty-coffee aroma drifted out. Vip felt Olive tense her claws on his shoulders, and he spun round at the sound of footsteps. He looked for somewhere to hide and crawled under the table with Olive on his back. He squeezed himself against a large box full of old towels as Fenella Stardust and Veronica Cheese walked into the room.

"You've left the star-key in the door, you stupid girl!" yelled Veronica Cheese. "It's wide open. Anyone could have walked in."

"I don't believe it," muttered Fenella Stardust, her hand flying up to where the star-key usually dangled around her neck. "I've never done that before. It must be the pressure of the live TV show. I've got too much to think about—"

"Well, if anyone finds out what's going on down here then there won't be any more TV shows!" snapped the old woman.

196

"Sorry, Mummy."

"When I think of everything I've given to you to make you famous," she continued. "And you can't even be bothered to lock this place up and keep it a secret. One silly mistake and your career could be over. The public will hate you!"

Fenella Stardust shuddered. "Don't say that, Mummy. It's safe down here. No one comes. It's strictly forbidden."

Veronica Cheese's shiny high heels clicked furiously past Vip's hiding place. Very slowly he reached for one of the old towels and pulled it over himself and Olive. He peeped out to see Fenella Stardust fiddling with her frilly blouse.

"Mummy?" she began.

"What is it? Can't you see I'm busy?" Veronica Cheese was standing over the bubbling cauldron and stirring it with a large wooden spoon.

"I've been thinking ... about retiring," murmured Fenella Stardust. "I'm sixty-five next year and—"

SLAM!

Vip and Olive jumped at the sound of the wooden

spoon being banged down on the table. "Don't you dare even say it!" shrieked Veronica Cheese. "You are my daughter and you will be famous for ever!"

"OK, OK. It was just a thought."

Veronica Cheese glared at her daughter for a whole minute before returning to the cauldron and stirring again.

"How long has this been simmering?" she demanded.

"Twelve hours. It should be ready."

"And you've used all the correct ingredients?"

"Of course – six kilos of carrots, two jars of coffee, a pinch of cocoa and six packets of stardust."

"I think we need an extra bag of stardust tonight," said Veronica Cheese.

Vip watched as she picked up one of the hair bags and sprinkled the contents into the cauldron. "Did you manage to get the cat's stardust?"

"No. I tried but—"

"Stupid girl! Animal stardust is ten times more powerful than human. That was top-quality stuff and the cat was covered in it. Those tiny particles of star-quality would have really boosted your performance tomorrow. Look at the state of you. Your voice is croaky, you have a wrinkle near your mouth and I'm sure I can see a grey hair. What a shame you never produced any of your own stardust. You haven't got a talented bone in your body."

Fenella Stardust drooped. "And to think that some people try to get rid of it," she murmured. "They think it's just flakes of skin – dandruff. There's even a shampoo which destroys it."

Vip listened closely. So that was why she wanted Olive so badly.

"Fools," said Veronica Cheese. "You're so lucky that I discovered what it really was when I was working in Hollywood. If I hadn't taken some for myself and sprinkled it on my talentless daughter, you would have been a nobody. You owe me everything."

"Yes, Mummy. Thank you, Mummy."

"What would you do without me? Even this academy was my idea. Those hair-vacuumers give you an endless supply of stardust. That Gerry Chalk ran out of it too quickly. Still, I suppose you put him to good use at the school."

"I didn't want him to be penniless," murmured Fenella Stardust.

Vip was finding it hard to take in all this information.

"You're too kind," said Veronica Cheese, hauling the cauldron on to the table above Vip. "OK, it's ready. Have you got the American-tan tights?"

Vip wasn't quite sure what was happening on the table above him. He was too scared to move a muscle. Olive lay still, occasionally looking up at him. It sounded like the mixture in the cauldron was being strained through the tights into a mixing bowl. He could hear the metal canisters being opened and the mixture pouring in.

"Put on your paper pants and vest and get into the tanning booth," said Veronica Cheese, pointing to the glass shower cubicle. "And make sure you turn around when the fake tan sprays out. You don't want any streaks."

"I know how to do it, Mummy," complained Fenella Stardust. "I do it every day."

"But tomorrow is special," she said. "And my child is going to outshine everyone else's."

Vip couldn't believe his ears. He finally understood what Fenella Stardust was up to. She was stealing tiny particles of star-quality from her students and using it in her fake tan to cover herself in their talent. No wonder Melody was feeling exhausted, and goodness knows how many other students. Vip clenched his jaw. He had to tell everyone. He had to pluck up the courage and stand up in front of those TV cameras and tell the world what a fraud Fenella Stardust really was.

19

Escape

Fenella Stardust emerged from the tanning booth shining like a highly polished tangerine. Vip peered out from under the table to see her studying her reflection in one of the many mirrors. She was holding her arms out to the side and bending her legs to dry her body. Tiny luminous flecks glinted from her skin – the stardust. Her mother nodded in approval.

"Make sure you're completely dry before getting dressed," she said. "You don't want to stain your clothes."

"I know, Mummy," she sighed. "Can you get the hairdryer for me? It's in a box under the table."

Veronica Cheese bent down and rummaged under the table. The hairs on Vip's arms pricked to attention as she pulled off the towel and looked him straight in the eye. With a sharp intake of breath she reached for his ear and pulled him out. Olive crept back under the towel unnoticed.

Fenella Stardust gasped in horror. "How long have you been there?" she demanded, grabbing a pink, fluffy dressing gown. "What have you heard?"

"N-nothing," stuttered Vip.

"Liar!" shouted Veronica Cheese. "He's heard everything. He knows our secret."

Fenella Stardust screwed up her face and looked like she was about to cry.

"What are we going to do?" she wailed.

"We haven't got time to do anything now," said her mother. "We have to prepare for the show. We'll have to keep him down here till after it's finished, then we can think of what to do with him tomorrow night."

"Everyone will wonder where he is. His parents will be here."

Veronica Cheese snorted like an angry dragon. "We could say that he's run away," she huffed. "Everyone knows the only reason he's here is because of the cat . . . the cat . . . where is it?"

Vip glanced furtively down at the table. He could see Olive's long black tail poking out from under the towel. "Asleep in my trailer," he said.

The old lady's eyes narrowed as they swept around the room. "Will she perform without the boy?" she asked.

Fenella Stardust shook her head.

"Then you will have to find a replacement act. Come along. The show must go on, and we have lots to sort out before tomorrow morning. Costumes, hair, sound, lighting, sets and. . ." she glared at Vip and pushed her long, taloned thumb into the palm of her other hand, ". . . an annoying little worm that needs to be squashed."

Veronica Cheese opened the door and beckoned to her daughter. Vip noticed a little black shadow flit behind her and dash out of the room. He sighed with relief. At least Olive was safe. Fenella Stardust glared at him as she walked towards her mother. "You could have ruined everything," she said, slamming the door behind her.

Vip breathed deeply to try and calm his pounding heart. What were they going to do with him when they returned? He had to escape before that happened and tell everyone the truth. He looked around the room and tried the door but it was locked firmly. He checked the walls for air vents and paced up and down trying to find any holes, cracks or gaps that might lead outside. He went back to the locked door and began banging it with all his might, shouting for help at the top of his voice. But he was deep underground, far away from the rest of the school.

Vip spent several fruitless hours thinking of a way out. Eventually his tired eyes rested on the brick fireplace. The only escape route was up the chimney. A triangle of flames still licked the grate. He looked around for a sink or tap or some water of any kind, but all he could see was the large cauldron which was still sitting on the table. There was a small amount of fake tan left in the bottom. He heaved the cauldron across the room and tipped the contents out over the fire. A monstrous hissing noise filled the chimney breast as the flames morphed into great clouds of orange smoke. The smell of burnt carrots was overwhelming. Vip knew that thick smoke was lethal. It would clog his lungs and kill him quicker than any fire. He looked at the smouldering remnants. It was going to be quite a while before the smoke cleared and the chimney grew cool enough to touch. He paced back and forth in frustration, but there was nothing he could do but sit in front of the fireplace and wait. As he watched, his eyelids grew heavier as the thick smoke slowly faded into wisps and shadows until they eventually disappeared completely. Vip tentatively touched the tiles in front of the grate. They were hot, which meant the chimney breast would still be like an oven. He realized that it would take a lot longer for the chimney to cool and he wouldn't be able to escape for another few hours. *I mustn't go to sleep*, he thought. *I must be ready by morning.* He wrapped an old towel around him and rested his head on the warm hearth.

"Wake up!"

Vip opened his eyes to see his parents standing by the door. They were holding the identical singing wombats that belonged to the twins in the third year.

"Mum!" he shouted. "Dad! What are you doing here . . . why have you got wombats?"

"Vip," said Dad, closing the door behind him. "Fenella Stardust told us that you weren't trying hard enough at school. Don't let us down."

"Don't believe anything she tells you," cried Vip. "She's a liar!"

"She wants to help you become a V-I-P," said Mum, holding up a packet of stardust. "A very important person."

There was a knock at the door. "That's her," said Dad. "She's going to turn you into a 'somebody'."

Knock, knock, knock!

"Don't let her in!" Vip yelled. "You have to help me. HELP ME!"

Vip sat bolt upright in front of the fireplace. He was sweating. The dream had felt so real it was hard to disentangle himself. He could still hear the pounding on the door.

Knock, knock, knock!

He leapt to his feet as he realized that this time the knocking was real.

"VIP!" cried a voice.

It was Melody.

20

Fenella Stardust's
Showbiz Extravaganza

The door clicked open and Melody stood there with the star-key in one hand and Olive in the other.

"How did you find me?" gasped Vip.

"Olive brought me here," she panted. "Everyone's in the Celebrity Circus Tent, students, parents and guests. Fenella Stardust had Olive on her shoulder, which was weird, and she told us all that you hadn't shown up and were going to be replaced by Gunter Gruber. Your parents think you're hiding because of the TV show and are going to reappear afterwards. Your dad is fuming. Then Olive jumped off Ms Stardust and on to my lap and dropped the key in

209

my hand. I suddenly realized why she was on her shoulder in the first place. Fenella Stardust doesn't have a clue. She thinks Olive likes her now. I knew exactly where you were then. I slipped out and ran down here as fast as I could."

"Has the show started?" asked Vip.

"Yes, it's nearly midday. Chardonnay Frontage was on first thing and Steven Stolid has been sucking his toes for the whole morning. I've performed already and Perry's on in a minute." She stopped and looked around the room. "What's going on down here?"

Vip spilled out the events of last night.

"What a cheating old fraud," spluttered Melody.

"I know," agreed Vip, "and I have to tell everyone."

They made their way back through the basement and outside to the Celebrity Circus Tent. Vip peeped through the door. All the seats were full. Perry was on the stage in the middle. He was sitting next to his large tub of soapy water, completely enclosed in a bubble, pretending to have a fight with Conker. Everyone was laughing, including Fenella Stardust who was standing behind him, well away from the water, but still in camera shot. To the side of the stage a glamorous lady who Vip recognized as Chardonnay Frontage was standing beside a stocky young man who was watching the proceedings whilst sucking his toes. Bright lights filled the circus ring with several camera crews racing around filming Perry and the audience's reaction. Vip could feel his legs growing weak. There was no way he would be able to get up in front of all these people.

"I can't do it," he said to himself.

He could see his parents in the front row. They were not laughing. Dad had his arms folded and Mum looked like she was about to cry. Vip felt a pang. They would have been looking forward to this show so much. It was a chance for him to be on TV. He would have been famous for five minutes. They looked so disappointed.

"You haven't let them down, Vip," said Melody gently. "There are other ways to be a very important person, you know. Now get on that stage and tell everyone the truth."

She leant forward and gave him a little push. The warmth from her fingers seemed to charge him with an invisible force. He took a deep breath and walked into the Celebrity Circus Tent. Perry stopped his play fight and his bubble popped when he saw Vip approaching the stage. Fenella Stardust's pencilled eyebrows shot up in alarm. Vip could see Veronica Cheese at the side of the stage pulling her hand across her throat in a gesture to cut the filming. But the cameras kept rolling. This was a live TV show.

"V-Vip Locks," cried Fenella Stardust.

Now she knows my name, thought Vip.

"So nice of you to join us at last . . . and you've brought your amazing cat, Olive."

There was a smattering of applause, but the audience realized that this wasn't planned. However, Vip's mum and dad were clapping loud enough for everyone.

"Go on, my son!" yelled Dad.

"Break a leg," shrieked Mum.

"You can do it," shouted Conker.

Vip glanced at Perry, who winked at him.

"I h-have s-something to t-tell everyone," began Vip. He wasn't sure if anyone could hear him over the thumping of his heart.

"How nice," said Fenella Stardust, trying to lead him off the stage. "But maybe later—"

"Let him talk," cried Dad, stepping on to the stage and smiling at the camera. "That's my boy."

Fenella Stardust let go of Vip and glanced anxiously at her furious mother.

"F-Fenella Stardust is stealing from the students of this academy," blurted Vip.

The audience gasped. Dad's knees gave way and he sat down where he stood.

"Very funny, Vip" said Fenella Stardust, looking nervously around. "Mr Chalk, if you wouldn't mind helping me here. I think Vip is a little overwhelmed by appearing on television . . . bless him."

Vip watched Mr Chalk come shuffling towards the stage.

"You have to believe me," cried Vip. "She's

213

stealing stardust – tiny particles of star quality, and covering herself in it. She's taking the students' talents for herself."

"Ha ha!" laughed Fenella Stardust. "I think we've found a new comedian here ... Mr Chalk would you please—"

"It's the hair-vacuumers," continued Vip, as Mr Chalk approached them. "They suck out the stardust."

Dad slunk off the stage and Mum hid her head in her hands as the audience began to boo.

"Get that boy off," shouted someone.

"He's ruining the show," cried another.

Mr Chalk stretched out his arms for Vip.

"M-Mr Chalk, it's true," sniffed Vip. "She stole from you too."

The old caretaker stepped forward. "I believe you, Vip," he said. "I took a closer look at that incinerator."

And he pushed Fenella Stardust into Perry's tub of bubble mixture.

*

Fenella Stardust fell into the tub with a huge splash, and was completely submerged by the soapy water. Everyone was on their feet, unsure now if this was all part of an act for the cameras. Veronica Cheese dashed up as Fenella Stardust emerged from the pool. Streaks of fake tan ran down her face, revealing her pale liver-spotted skin beneath. As the tan containing the stardust washed off, she appeared to shrivel like a slug in salt water. Her spiky black hair greyed and thinned, falling limply over her face.

"NOOOOOOOOOO!!!!!" she screamed.

But her smooth, velvety voice had been replaced by a ragged croak. Everyone watched in stunned silence as a bent and scraggy Fenella Stardust stood before them.

21

A Cheat
and a Fraud

Mr Chalk pulled Fenella Stardust out of the tub of soapy water. "The boy is telling the truth," he shouted. "I have seen the proof with my own eyes. Fenella Stardust has lied to me and to you, and is stealing your children's talent."

There was an angry shout from one of the parents, and some of them began to boo again but this time it was directed at Fenella Stardust. She looked like she was going to faint.

"She took my stardust too," continued Mr Chalk, "ruined my career and pretended to be my friend. She is a cheat and a fraud!"

Fenella Stardust covered her ears as the booing increased.

"I'm so sorry," she cried. "I had to do it. My mother was desperate for me to be famous."

Vip knew exactly how that felt. He looked across at the sagging old woman and began to feel sorry for her. They had more in common than he had realized.

"You ungrateful child," yelled Veronica Cheese. "You love being famous."

"I love being loved," admitted Fenella Stardust. "But it's exhausting too."

The booing got louder and more ferocious.

"Please forgive me," she continued, "especially you, Gerry."

Mr Chalk was still holding Fenella Stardust up by her arms. He released her but the angry furrows ploughed across his forehead.

"You have nothing to be sorry for," shouted Veronica Cheese above the booing. "Why shouldn't you take a little bit of stardust? Most of the students didn't even notice and some of them went on to have successful careers. Chardonnay Frontage and Steven Stolid are proof of that."

She pointed at the two celebrities who were watching in shock from the side of the stage.

"But, I used to be able to play the trumpet," said Chardonnay Frontage.

"So did I," cried Steven Stolid, "with my toes!"

"I am a cheat," sobbed Fenella Stardust. "I took most of your talent and all of Mr Chalk's. I don't want to be famous any more. I've had enough. Everybody hates me."

"Rubbish!" shrieked Veronica Cheese. "No publicity is bad publicity! Don't throw it all away. You're still famous! You can do whatever you like – eat pus-filled grubs in a forest, pretend to be best friends with other famous people, write forty-seven autobiographies and a children's book! Don't become a 'nobody'. Remember, what does fame mean?"

Fenella Stardust looked around the jeering crowd and a large teardrop trickled down her withered cheek.

"Nothing," she whispered.

"You are pathetic!" spat Veronica Cheese. "I have devoted myself to turning you into a 'somebody', you idiot, and if I say you're going to be famous then—"

"Leave her alone!" cried Vip.

The booing died down and everyone turned to look at him. The cameraman to his left zoomed in on his face but Vip didn't care. He was fed up with all this nonsense about "somebodies" and "nobodies" and suddenly felt very angry.

"Who cares if she's famous or not?" he shouted. "She's still your daughter."

Veronica Cheese's taut face creased into a nasty scowl. "You have no idea what you're talking about," she sneered. "Fame brings you wealth, happiness and love."

"She doesn't look very happy to me," answered Vip, looking at the shrivelled Fenella Stardust. "And it's not real love. What good is money without the other two?"

"Fame is the ultimate goal!" she shrieked.

"Being good at what you do should be your

219

goal," he argued, "and that might bring you fame. But what's the point in trying to be famous just for the sake of it?"

The old woman looked ready to explode but Vip carried on talking. It was as if a tap had been turned on and he couldn't stop it. "I don't care if I've got mousy-brown hair and don't stand out. I don't want to stand out! I don't care if I'm no good at performing. I never want to see another stage in my life! And I don't care if I'm too quiet. I like being QUIET!"

Everybody stared at him in stunned silence, including his mum and dad. Vip looked down at them. "I just want to be me," he said. "I've tried telling you a million times, but you never listen."

Somebody at the back of the tent began to clap. Vip turned to see Melody walking towards him. Then Perry stepped up beside him with Conker's little wooden hands tapping together. Dwayne left his seat and joined them on the stage, clapping loudly. Soon Cherry and Merlin joined in, closely followed by Pineapple, Gunter, Ben and Howl.

"V-I-P," chanted Cherry, producing her golden pom-poms. "V-I-P."

Vip watched in amazement as one by one the whole audience got to their feet and began applauding. All except Veronica Cheese.

"Idiots!" she yelled. But everyone, including her own daughter, ignored her.

Vip was suddenly surrounded by the smell of *He-Man* aftershave and pork-and-apple sausages, as his mum and dad climbed on to the stage and hugged him.

"We're so sorry, Vip," sniffed Mum. "It must have taken a lot of guts to get up here and expose Fenella Stardust."

"And even more to defend her when everyone was booing," added Dad. "We're so proud of you, son."

Vip felt giddy and hugged them back. His dad had never said that before. They emerged from their huddle to the sound of a microphone being turned on. Fenella Stardust stood in centre stage. Her soggy, sequinned dress had lost its sparkle and hung

221

from her bent body. She grabbed the microphone with a gnarled hand.

"I have m-made some terrible mistakes," she croaked, "and would like to make a formal apology to all students, past and present. I cannot return your stardust, but the more you practise your own special skills, the more stardust you will produce. So if you carry on practising then your talents will return. I know that I don't deserve your forgiveness, especially my old friend Mr Gerry Chalk. But if you will allow me, I would like to make up for my past misdemeanours. After listening to Vip, I have a new vision for this school which I would like to discuss with all students, parents and staff." She looked directly at the head cameraman. "So from today, Stardust Academy is a wrap!"

22

A Very Important Person

Vip had the best Christmas ever. Mum and Dad had bought him a book called *The Vital Veterinary Guide*, which he read every day. They had even given him a real stethoscope so that he could listen to Olive's and Henry the hamster's heartbeats. Olive sat on his shoulder as he checked the book and the stethoscope were safely in his bag. He was looking forward to getting back to school after the Christmas break, and walked happily up to the big golden gates with his mum and dad.

"Well, look at that," said Dad, pointing up at the gates. The large Stardust Academy sign had been taken down and replaced with another one.

"The Chalk and Cheese School for Excellence," he read.

Crowds of children were waiting outside with their parents.

"Phenomen-omen-omen-omen-omenal!" cried a familiar voice.

Vip turned to see Cherry with her arm around Pineapple. They were spinning round and round on their toes, obviously delighted to be starting a new term. Howl was just behind them, talking to Gunter, who was hooting and yodelling with laughter. Ben somersaulted in with his parents cartwheeling behind, and Merlin suddenly appeared from nowhere. Most of the older students were there too, but they had been joined by lots of new faces. Perry, Melody and Dwayne came running towards Vip.

"Hurry up, Vip," shouted Melody. "They're opening the gates."

A man came out of the school building followed by a large group of teachers. Vip could see that it was Mr Chalk. His slicked-back hair was shining like silver and he was looking very dapper in a smart suit. Following behind the group was a woman in a blue dress and a matching fake-fur hat.

"Look, it's Fenella Stardust," he whispered. "She looks older."

"She looks better," added Perry.

Fenella Stardust did look older – and better. Her silk dress shimmered subtly in the winter sunshine.

"*Lady in blue. . .*" trilled Dwayne.

Her skin had lost its taut orange hue and now fell into comfortable creases around her face. Vip thought she looked wiser and much more distinguished. She smiled and waved at him as the golden gates swung open.

"Welcome, everybody, to the Chalk and Cheese School for Excellence!" she shouted. "After persuading Mr Chalk to take to the stage once more, we were pleasantly surprised to discover that his skills as a performer have recovered and he will now be in charge of performing arts."

Mr Chalk did a little tap dance which was greeted with lots of cheering.

"Thanks to the suggestions made by our very own Vip Locks," continued Fenella Stardust, "we will now be covering a much wider range of subjects."

Vip wasn't sure where to look as lots of students chanted his name and slapped him on the back.

"From Latin dancers to Latin linguists, mad magicians to mathematicians, wombat breeders to avid readers," she said, "we are here to help you achieve your personal goal, whatever that may be."

"No dream is too extreme!" shouted Mr Robust from the line of teachers.

"Oh dear, he's still here," muttered Perry.

"He's not so bad," said Vip, "But I wonder what my personal trainers will be like this term?"

"I think they'll be a lot more confident," answered Melody. "I doubt they'll run away any more, although they might still go red every now and then."

Vip's cheeks began to tingle again, so he quickly changed the subject. "Look, there's Dr Doolots," he said. "Mr Van Driver is here too and so is Mr

Poser-Prince. But I can't see Miss Maykova, and there are lots of new teachers that I don't recognize at all."

"Who's that hiding behind Fenella Stardust?" asked Melody. "Oh no, I don't believe it."

They all stepped back in astonishment as Veronica Cheese appeared. Her arms were folded and her lips were turned down in a sullen sulk. Fenella Stardust ushered her forward.

"Could all the mums and dads who are attending our 'Rehabilitation Course for Pushy Parents', please come with me," she said.

The old woman stomped behind her as she headed towards a new building set up in the grounds. Perry's mum was at the back of a large group of parents following them. "Shouldn't we have vaccinations if we're all going to be in the same room as each other?" she asked.

"You'll be fine, Mum," called Perry. "Give it a go."

Vip said goodbye to his mum and dad as they joined them. "Just try your best," he said.

"We will," answered Mum.

"We're going to be the best un-pushiest parents ever!" shouted Dad.

Melody's mother kissed her goodbye and hurried up the hill after them. "I think you'll find that I am going to be the best un-pushiest parent around here," she said.

They waved them all goodbye as Mr Chalk handed out some new school timetables.

"We've all got English and maths together," said Melody, studying the timetable. "Then I've got violin practice after lunch. What are you three doing?"

Perry covered Conker's ears. "Woodwork and working with wood," he whispered.

"Operatic acrobatics!" sang Dwayne.

Vip looked down at his timetable and gasped in delight. "Animal biology. Brilliant!"

Melody linked arms with the boys and pulled them towards the school. "I can't wait to get started," she said. "Everyone is going to get a chance to be really good at whatever they want to do and it's all thanks to you, Vip. You've changed everything."

Vip felt his cheeks flush but he didn't mind. That was just who he was – slightly shy, easily embarrassed . . . but still a Very Important Person.

SIOBHAN ROWDEN was born in Scotland and brought up in England. She has a degree in English and has worked as a holiday rep in Corfu, at Disney World in Florida and for a production company in London. *The Curse of the Bogle's Beard* was her first novel followed by *Revenge of the Ballybogs* and *Wild Moose Chase*. She lives in Brighton with her husband and children. She doesn't like blue cheese.

www.siobhanrowden.com
@SiobhanRowden